STOLEN MAGE BRIDE

STOLEN BRIDES OF THE FAE

SYLVIA MERCEDES

© 2021 by Sylvia Mercedes

Published by FireWyrm Books

www.SylviaMercedesBooks.com

Cover image by Dominique Wesson

Title Text by Sarah KL Wilson

Dedicated to my two dragon babies.
I can't wait to hold you both in my arms!
But it was fun to feel you wriggling inside of me while I wrote
this tale.

LODÍRHAL, KING OF AURELIS

"**M**y king, the humans have answered your challenge. They've agreed to the terms of the Champion Combat."

My seneschal's words reach me as though from a great distance. I feel them scratch at the back of my awareness like hounds at the door, but for the moment I refuse to let them in. Instead, I draw another slow breath low in my gut. As I let it out, I feel the swell of magic in my veins, drawn up from the deep places in my soul.

I need all the magic I can gather for what is coming next.

At one time, long ago when the thin air of this human world did not thicken my blood to such a sluggish flow, I had no need to enter a meditative state to summon my own power. I was strong then. Strong enough to conjure illusions that sent entire companies of human soldiers fleeing in terror before me.

But now, as one by one the spires of Eledria have

fallen and my people have lost their grip on this world, my magic fades.

I feel the pressure of Lord Enbalar's gaze on the back of my head. I must give an answer.

"Very well." The words fall unhurried from my lips. "Send for my obligates to array me for battle."

Tension tightens the atmosphere. Enbalar does not like this plan.

As I slowly twist to look back, the last traces of my hard-won serenity disperse like untethered magic into the ether, and my hands, pressed in an attitude of prayer before my heart, drop to rest on my knees.

At sight of Enbalar standing just inside the tent flap, I frown. Sometimes I forget how critically his magic has faded over the last few months. The layers of glamour he usually wears like his own skin have eroded, revealing the truth beneath—the ugly purple scar across one cheek that twists the shape of his mouth. The milkiness of a damaged eye. War has taken a dreadful toll on this mighty lord of Aurelis.

But then, we have all paid that toll.

"Speak, Enbalar." My voice betrays none of the roiling tension in my breast. "I would rather hear your protests than endure one moment more of your battering silence."

"My king." Enbalar bows his head, placing a hand over his heart. "Why not wait a little longer? The reinforcements from Noxaur must arrive any day. Kyriakos will not fail you. He owes you too great a debt."

"You hope too much of our friend Kyriakos." Unfolding my legs, I rise and turn to face my seneschal.

"He need only invent a fine excuse or two, delay no more than a day . . . and by the time he reaches this shore, we will be slaughtered. Then he and his jackals will pick our bones clean."

Enbalar's cheeks drain of color. "But are you certain this single combat you propose is the best choice? We cannot afford to lose you."

"Is your faith in your king so frail? I intend to win."

"But you know what they will do!" Enbalar's voice loses its hesitation as urgency takes over. "Those Miphates will send their Warrior. They will send Ilestriesa. She is their champion, and she is . . . she is . . ."

Although the words trail off, I hear his unspoken fears like tolling bells.

She is *spectacular*.

She is *terrible*.

She is *death*.

And he is right. I've seen the Incarnate Warrior. Once. At a great distance. More than a century ago, as humans count the passage of time. Back when she was carried by a different Vessel. At sight of her, I wanted to charge through the ranks and challenge her, cut her down with a sweep of my sword.

But I saw how she moved with the grace and poise of a dancer, her battleaxes twirling in deadly arcs of silver. I witnessed the way raw magic flowed from her in wave after wave of brilliant, soul-slicing light that left my people broken, their corpses warped beyond recognition. I beheld the matchless strength of her when she turned her attention suddenly skyward to where Queen Elase-tora circled overhead astride her great red dragon.

The Incarnate Warrior took one look at that dragon, then gathered herself and leapt straight into the air. With one mighty hand, she caught the dragon by its throat and ripped it from the sky. Its body smote the ground with a reverberation that caused soldiers on both sides of the battle to fall on their faces in dismay. Ilestriesa, undaunted, cleaved the dragon's skull with one ax and with the other removed Queen Elasetora's head in a single blow.

So the fae withdrew from the land of Vaaly. And one of our great towers, the Nearspire, fell into mortal hands.

After that battle, no one saw or heard of Ilestriesa. Some said that before it died the dragon bit her Vessel, a nameless mortal magess who soon afterward succumbed to its venom, leaving the spirit of Ilestriesa without a Vessel.

However, less than a year ago, word reached me that a new Vessel had been found, trained by the thrice-cursed Miphates, and taught to bear the burden of the Incarnate Warrior. And yesterday I witnessed her arrival. She stood across the battleground, a small, distant figure, unprepossessing at first glance . . . yet the Warrior Spirit's aura was unmistakable.

She has come. The war is over.

Unless . . . unless . . .

"It's not too late, my king."

With an effort I wrench myself from these dark thoughts as my seneschal takes a step toward me. "Your people are brave," Enbalar says. "We are ready, we are willing to fight this battle. We do not ask you to die in our stead."

So much fear glimmers in his eyes. Once upon a time, I would never have believed any fae lord would fear a mere human enemy. But after nearly two hundred years of war—of watching the humans drive us from our conquered lands one slow, bloody inch at a time—fear has crept in, insidious as a cancer. I feel it too. Deep down.

But fear can be useful. I shall channel it, tame it, and use it to augment my waning power. I can master this emotion, just like any other.

"My friend," I say, resting a hand on Enbalar's shoulder. "For too long now, we've watched our brothers and sisters fall. And although each of their deaths costs a hundred of our enemy's lives in return, the human ranks never diminish. Wave upon wave of carcasses they send to die on our swords until we are crushed beneath the sheer weight of them. They are no match for us save in numbers alone—but their numbers are terrible." My words are bitter, but I continue, speaking the truth neither of us wants to admit. "We cannot withstand another melee."

"Then we should retreat." Enbalar rests his hand on my forearm, his grip trembling. "Aurelis already lost your father . . . we cannot lose another king. If we are to rebuild, if we are to remain strong among the kingdoms of Eledria, we must have *you*. So, give the mortals their victory. Don't sacrifice your life to Ilestriesa."

"And what of the Evenspire?" I shake my head slowly without breaking Enbalar's gaze. "It is the last of our strongholds in this land. Should we lose it, we lose all— the kingdom, the war. This entire world." My jaw hardens. "I cannot let it go without a fight. But I will not see my people slaughtered. No! I will face their champion. I will face their Warrior. And I will vanquish her."

Enbalar looks stricken, but he does not press his argument. Instead, he bows his head and, with no more than a murmured, "Your will is my command," exits the tent. The next moment, I hear him call out to my servants.

Minutes later, the tent flap opens, and two obligates—humans indentured to my service—enter, carrying my shining gold-plated armor. I hold out my arms for them to begin their work. They drape me first in delicately wrought chainmail, then affix the other pieces. I reject the bulky pauldrons and greaves, even the helmet, opting for a lighter, quicker battle array. If I'm to face Ilestriesa, armor will provide little protection. Ours will be a contest of magic, of sheer power and sheer will, not of armor and blades.

Their job complete, the obligates step back, heads bowed. Do they secretly rejoice behind those demure expressions? Pleased that their master must surely go to his doom?

Let them think what they will, hope what they will. I'm not dead yet.

I sweep back the flap and stride out into the morning, relieved to escape the shadowy tent. Though the sun of this world is pale and weak, I lift my face to it, close my eyes, and drink in the light like a draught of spring water.

When I open my eyes again, I find my people, armed for battle, surrounding me. All these loyal faces, the last of my great force. Hollow-eyed yet clinging to the last vestiges of their glamours. Their armor shines, their weapons gleam. Their eyes are bright, ferocious.

These are good people. My people. People worth dying for.

"My king! King Lodírhal!"

Turning sharply, I see the crowd part to make way for Enbalar. My seneschal throws himself to the ground at my knees and clasps my hand tight. "The reinforcements from Noxaur! They are here!"

"What?" I look over Enbalar's head down to the shore of the peninsula we fight to defend. Sure enough, on the horizon, black sails appear in the hazy distance. I narrow my eyes, drawing on magic to sharpen my vision, and can just discern flags bearing the insignia of Kyriakos, Lord of Ninthalor.

My heart catches in my throat.

"We're saved." Enbalar lifts his face, his eyes bright with the first gleam of hope I've seen in some time. "Call off this Champion Combat. With Kyriakos, we have a chance, a true chance of winning the day, of driving these mortals from the Evenspire once and for all."

For a moment—a painful, brilliant, heart-pounding moment—I hesitate. The temptation is strong.

But if I retract the challenge now, what message does it send to my people, to the humans? Only that the King of Aurelis is a coward.

Without acknowledging my seneschal's plea, I step around him and march through the small town of tents pitched around the base of the Evenspire. The soldiers of Aurelis fall in behind, following me to the edge of our encampment where the field of battle lies. Not seven days ago, this was a broad green swath of open country. Now it's a trampled horror of mud and blood.

Across the way stands the human army. A wall of bodies two thousand strong, armed with lances that glitter like teeth in the morning light. Even as I watch, the wall parts to admit a small party on horseback onto the field. Three riders wearing the flowing robes of Miphates, mortal mages. The one in the center is a woman.

"My horse!" I call out.

My white steed is brought, and I mount. Enbalar and Lady Tephysea of Teriani appear on either side of me, ready to ride out to meet the Miphates. Enbalar's face is deathly pale, but Lady Tephysea offers me a stern, approving nod. She would never forgive me if I backed out of this fight.

Together we enter the field. The very field where we've fought, suffered, and watched our comrades die over the last terrible weeks. Silence holds the world captive. I hear nothing beyond the pounding beat of my own heart. We draw nearer, nearer—close enough that I begin to distinguish details of the three approaching Miphates.

To my right rides an old man with a flowing white beard. He wears the purple and saffron of the Myrdin Order, and gold embroidery on his hood bespeaks his exalted rank. The mage to my left is younger, taller, an angular man with eyes like knives. He rides with his hood cast back over his shoulders, and his robe is as red as blood. One of the violent Uladir Order, then.

As the gap between us closes, I turn my gaze to the central mage. The woman. The Vessel of the Warrior.

Like the Uladir mage, her head is uncovered. Her dark hair is swept back from her face with blue ribbons, falling over her shoulders in long, glossy coils. She wears the green and silver robes of the Olorie Order. Which is surprising. Am I mistaken? The Olorie Order, unique among human magicians, is known for its peaceful ways and love of growing things. In all my years of campaigning, I've never faced an Olorie in battle.

The girl lifts her face slightly. How young she is! Young and fresh-faced and soft. But this makes sense—she has only recently risen through the ranks, training to bear the weight of Ilestriesa's glory. Youth means inexperience. Which is encouraging. My heart lifts for the first time that morning. I'm a seasoned warrior, after all. Maybe I have a chance.

Suddenly, the girl's eyelids flicker and rise. She gazes across the field, straight at me. I glimpse pure blue irises, the same shade of blue as the crystalline sky above. Her eyes flash as though with their own inner light, and for a moment . . . for a moment . . .

A sensation like an arrow pierces my heart.

My body tenses, every muscle contracting painfully, leaving me paralyzed. Worse still, deep in my soul, sudden heat blazes into an inferno so fierce that I fear it will burst through my chest, leaving me scorched and hollow. I lose all sense of self, time, space, even existence, utterly lost in excruciating pain.

Then I blink.

I lie on my back.

On my back, in the middle of the battlefield.

Staring at the sky above me.

A sky the same color as the young Miphata's eyes.

"Lodírhal!" Enbalar's voice. An indistinct form appears before my spinning vision, bowed over me with concern. "My king, what has happened? Did they curse you? Answer me!"

I cannot answer. Not yet. I cannot even breathe.

I stare beyond Enbalar's worried face at that distant sky. And slowly, slowly, understanding filters through the throbbing pain in my head.

It has found me.

It has found me at last.

The very thing I've dreaded all my life. The moment foretold by the soothsayer over my cradle, the prediction of my downfall, of my great and terrible weakness. The fear I've suppressed so deeply and for so long, I almost forgot it entirely. Until now. Until this moment.

That girl . . .

That mage, that monster, that mortal . . .

She is my Fated Love.

MAGE DASYRA ROLIM, VESSEL OF THE INCARNATE WARRIOR

*W*ell, that's certainly odd.

I rein my horse to a halt as I stare across the battlefield at the bizarre scene taking place. One moment, the magnificent fae king in his golden armor bore down upon me like doom itself. The next . . .

He is lying in the dirt. Spasming.

I glance to my left at Mage Jhaan, my master. Did he cast a curse? No, his eyes are widening behind their dense wrinkles and bristling brows. So I turn to Mage Glarald on my right, noting how his teeth flash in a grimace. Maybe he—

"What did you do?" Mage Jhaan turns in his saddle, directing his question over my head as though I'm not here. Typical.

Glarald shoots a ferocious glare at the older mage. "What did *I* do? What did *you* do, old man? That's no curse of mine."

Mage Jhaan huffs, his mouth working as though getting ready to spit. "I would never compromise the sacred laws of Champion Combat. But you . . . you were against this from the start. You were—"

"Esteemed Miphates!" It takes some courage to speak up, to insert myself between those two when they're bristling for battle. Their gazes swivel my way. "Remember, we are watched," I say, jutting my chin forward.

Both mages turn to where the fae king lies motionless after his bout of thrashing. A fae with a damaged beauty glamour has dismounted and kneels at his side. From this distance I can't hear what he says, but I feel the anxiety radiating from him. Whatever fit just possessed King Lodírhal has surprised his people as much as us.

While the fae lord's attention focuses on his fallen monarch, the lady fae, still astride her powerful gray mare, watches my fellow mages and me with glinting eyes. Her hand rests on the hilt of an undrawn sword. Even through its sheath I sense layer upon layer of deadly spells wrapping the blade.

"Dasyra," Mage Jhaan growls. I feel my master's gaze on the side of my face. He never bothers to honor me with the title *mage* that is my due, since he does not see me as a true mage. "Child, did you do something? Is this spell of your working? Are you trying to disrupt—"

Before he can finish his accusation, the fae lord bowed over the fallen king springs to his feet and whirls to face us, drawing his sword in a single sweeping motion. "Villains!" he cries in the strong lyrical accent I've come to associate with Aurelian fae. "You dare commit such treachery? Luring us out so you might cast your petty curses? You'll die like the dogs you are!"

He runs toward us then, losing all trace of his

faltering glamour. His unmasked face is broken, scarred, mangled, so unlike the usual image of fae perfection. He looks like a monster.

My heart thuds in my throat even as my hand reaches unconsciously for the amulet resting against my heart, beneath my robes. Jhaan and Glarald both draw written spells from hidden pockets up their long sleeves and begin to murmur the words of spellcasting, pulling power through the ether into this world.

In another few seconds, there will be bloodshed.

With a cry, I fling myself from my saddle. While my horse snorts and stamps, I avoid its hooves and rush out into the empty space between the mages and the oncoming fae. Spinning to face Jhaan and Glarald, I raise both arms. My back is exposed to the approaching fae and his sword, but the swelling power of the Miphates' spells is by far the worse threat.

"Stop!" I shout.

In the same moment, I feel Ilestriesa surge inside me with force that nearly knocks me to my knees. The need to catch hold of the amulet and summon her power threatens to overwhelm me. But no. No! I am more than a mere vessel.

I stare up into Jhaan's furious face illuminated by the harsh light of the spell roiling in the palm of his hand. Glarald's eyes are wide with shock, his own spell upraised and ready to hurl.

"Get out of the way, girl," Jhaan bellows.

I don't move. How close is the fae lord behind me? How many seconds do I have before his blade pierces my spine? I hold Jhaan's gaze, refusing to look down.

Another voice echoes across the field: *"Enbalar, phyra tor!"*

The tone of command is so strong, so overwhelming, I cannot resist the impulse to turn and look back over my shoulder. To my horror, I see the fae lord a mere five paces behind me— so close that I can see the milky brokenness of his damaged eye and the ugly stitches holding the flesh of his cheek and lip together.

But beyond him . . . oh, gods! Beyond him, gleaming like an angelic being in the light of the morning sun, Lodírhal the Magnificent stands upright. His hair flows like golden banners in the breeze, and his eyes are bright flames. His mouth is still open, the air rings with the sound of his voice, and the power of his spirit rolls out across the field, restraining the upraised sword of the fae lord, which is poised to hew into my skull.

No one—neither fae nor human—would dare ignore such a command.

"Stand down," Lodírhal repeats, this time speaking in my own tongue. "Return to me, Lord Enbalar. Do not break the lawful bonds of the Champion Combat. Stand down, I say."

The fae lord blinks once, his gaze still fixed on me with deep hatred. For an instant, however, I see a flicker of fear in his eye. Fear of me or of his master? It hardly matters which, for the effect is the same. He lowers his sword and, without a word, retreats to where his king and the lady fae on horseback wait.

I release a tightly held breath, then glance back at the two Miphates behind me. They're both lowering their spells, thank the gods, letting the power drift away through their fingertips. Jhaan's face is an expressionless mask of wrinkles. He jerks his chin sharply, summoning me back to my place. I duck my head and obey without a word. Now that the moment is past, I realize how my heart is pounding, how my knees tremble. I lack the strength to mount so merely catch my horse's reins and lean against its shoulder for support.

I glimpse movement across the field: Lodírhal again approaches, his lord and lady behind him. The shining power of his voice has faded, and . . . Do I imagine it, or does he look distinctly unwell? His face is pale, almost gray, and stark lines score his cheeks and brow. Something is definitely not right with him. Nevertheless, he is an imposing figure. And undeniably beautiful.

Warmth radiates across my cheeks. Am I blushing? Gods on high, how embarrassing!

It's not your fault, I remind myself quickly. *It's the influence of the fae glamours. That's all.*

Somehow, I don't quite believe it.

Lodírhal stands in the space halfway between the two armies, his feet planted, his head high. "Greetings, Miphates," he declares, raising a hand after Serythian fashion. "I come to honor the Champion Agreement. Declare your champion that we may fight."

Jhaan and Glarald exchange uneasy glances over my head. Then Jhaan, his mouth deeply downturned beneath his white froth of beard, takes the lead, urging his horse two paces forward. He does not dismount, for he's shorter than Lodírhal by more than a head. My old master would die before he made this fact apparent to all present.

15

"King Lodírhal of Aurelis," he says, sweeping an arm to indicate me. "We too are prepared to honor the terms of the Agreement. Let whoever draws first blood take the Evenspire. May the gods declare before all witnesses whom they deem worthy of this victory."

Smugness laces his voice. I frown, sick to my stomach. Jhaan knows exactly what Ilestriesa can and will do to this glorious fae being. He knows exactly how this battle will end.

At least . . . he thinks he knows.

You are more than a vessel. I grit my teeth and close my eyes. *You are more than what they've made of you.*

A few more words pass between the king and my master. Then, quite suddenly, the back-and-forth is complete. The courtly words and pretty speeches are done. And I face the moment I've dreaded since the night Ilestriesa chose me.

Glarald leads my horse away, leaving me standing in the field, small and exposed. Jhaan murmurs a few final words from the lofty safety of his saddle. I block out whatever he's saying and feel strangely relieved when he turns his mount's head and follows Glarald back toward our side of the battleground.

I watch them go, my throat dry and a little scratchy even though they're closer to enemies than friends. I loathe them almost as much as they despise me. But they're *my* people. They're part of *my* world.

Now they're gone. And only battle remains.

I turn to face the battlefield. The fae lord and lady have taken leave of their master and are hastening back to where the fae army stands opposite the human

16

soldiers. No one remains in the field but me and King Lodírhal.

And Ilestriesa.

For a moment I wonder: Can I simply refuse to summon the Warrior? After all, if I don't speak the words of the spell, I cannot be wholly indwelt. I could choose to face Lodírhal simply as myself.

A pitiful idea. I'm no match for a warrior like him. Me —a little Olorie magess. What do I imagine I can do on my own against the simmering power I sense roiling in the essence of his being?

And if I fail, what will that mean for my people? Only another day of slaughter. Of lives needlessly lost.

Drawing my spine straight as a spear, I look across the stretch. For half a second, my enemy meets my gaze. Then his eyes quickly swivel away from mine to focus anywhere else. Is he afraid?

He should be.

Lodírhal draws his sword. It flashes in the sunlight, Eledrian metal infused with magic that flows through it like blood through veins. He widens his stance, gripping the sword with both hands. His face is intent, but his eyes still won't focus on me.

Behind me, a murmuring chant begins. A low susurrus of sound slowly swells until I can hear the single word repeated again and again in time to the thud of lance butts hitting the soil: "*Ilestriesa. Ilestriesa. Ilestriesa.*"

I cannot delay. Not a moment longer.

It's time to summon their Warrior.

I reach inside the neckline of my gown and withdraw the amulet. The Heart of Ilestriesa, a beautiful thing of ancient days wrought with symbols etched into both sides of the flat stone. I don't need to read the symbols; I memorized them long ago. Yet I feel out each line, reading with my fingertips instead of my eyes.

"Ilestriesa, Ilestriesa, Ilestriesa," chant the soldiers at my back.

"Tanatar, wynal-ha," I whisper. *"Anaerin, mir yinthana, abore so thula—"*

By the darkness of Tanatar, and the mystery of Anaerin, I summon thee—

"ILESTRIESA!"

LODÍRHAL

*R*eality cracks.

I recoil a step. I can't help myself. The shock rippling through the worlds is so great that I barely keep from falling to my knees.

My eyes cannot see the shudder streaking through layers upon layers of worlds and realms, but I feel it—vividly, profoundly, with senses beyond ordinary perception. The spell bursting from the young woman's lips breaks from this world of mundane matter into a distant dimension.

The *quinsatra*. The realm of pure magic.

A stream of multi-colored light and energy pours into this world in a torrential flood, streaks like a waterfall from the sky, and strikes the amulet upraised in the young Miphata's hands. It breaks around her, streaming, radiating tremendous heat that undulates across the field in waves and threatens to knock me from my feet again.

Yet the girl stands there at its core. Cool, distant. Her spirit set apart.

Shading my eyes with one hand, I see the transformation overcoming her limbs. The delicate mortal maid is still there, just visible. But around her, the phantom spirit of the Warrior takes shape. A tremendous figure, like a woman but not quite. A being beyond such labels as manhood and womanhood, angelic, nearly godlike. Seven feet tall she stands, clad in armor of silver and light. Hair the color of moonlight wafts around a face as dark as living obsidian, set with eyes like two green gems.

Within the phantom's outline, the Miphata pulls her upraised hands apart. They are empty . . . but the Warrior's hands are not. Two massive battleaxes scythe on either side of her, so sharp they seem to slice through the air itself, trailing sparks of raw magic. With this motion, the Warrior's form solidifies, becoming more real while the Miphata becomes less.

Ilestriesa. The mighty. The terrible. The unstoppable.

She crosses her axes before her breast, lifts her chin, and gazes between the hafts straight at me. Straight into my trembling soul.

She smiles.

If I don't act now, I will lose all self-control, all reason.

A wordless cry bursting from my throat, I throw myself forward, my sword upraised. For a moment Ilestriesa makes no move, as though she simply waits for me to break across her like foam.

Then suddenly her right arm lashes out, her ax swinging straight for my knees. Trusting to fighting instincts honed over centuries, I spring straight up, just clearing the blade as it whistles beneath my feet. But she gives me no reprieve; her second ax hews downward in a stroke I just manage to block with my sword.

Still in midair, I kick out with one foot. Instead of armored boots, I wear light sandals strapped to my calves. The choice pays off: My heel connects with the Warrior's jaw, and I could swear I hear a small gasp burst, not from the Warrior's lips, but from the girl down inside her.

Interesting. So the Vessel herself may still be reached, even through this powerful enchantment.

Using the momentum of my kick, I backflip away from Ilestriesa, narrowly avoiding a riposte from her right-hand ax. I land on my feet, perfectly balanced despite the uneven terrain. Magic sears in my veins— natural magic awakened by my own imminent peril. It's a glorious sensation, akin to bloodlust.

But I have no time to revel. Ilestriesa bears down on me, her wild hair streaming like a storm in her wake. I set my weight firmly on my back foot and lunge, attempting to take the offensive. The reach of my sword is greater, but her axes move in a blur of light and *quinsatra* force, catching my blade between them and twisting. I have a split second to decide: fight to keep my grip and risk losing my balance or let go.

I release the hilt.

My sword flies high even as I drop low to the ground, balancing on my fingertips and the ball of one foot. My other leg sweeps out, hooking the Warrior at the heel and pulling her off-center. For a moment I feel the tremendous strength of her and fear I won't be able to break her stride.

But though the Warrior may be ancient, strong, and deadly, her Vessel—still present and not so deeply hidden as it seems—is slight and inexperienced.

Piercing through layers of magic, I shoot my awareness down to where the young Miphata is just discernable within the overwhelming power of Ilestriesa. It's *her* foot my outstretched leg found and knocked out from under her.

She falls flat on her face in the field. To onlookers it may seem as though the Warrior lies sprawled in the trampled grass, but in that moment the spell wavers, and I see only the girl.

I jump, land hard on her back, and press her into the ground. It's the work of an instant to wrap my arm around her neck, anchor my hold with my other arm, and squeeze. Ilestriesa tries to fight, but I force my magic perception through the spell, concentrating on the Vessel. I feel her shape morphing, becoming smaller, softer, unprotected by either armor or muscle. Warm and close and vulnerable beneath me. Her hands grip my choking arm, uselessly scrabbling, scratching, struggling to break my hold.

I reach for the knife sheathed at my thigh and slide it out. One short, sharp blow straight into her throat, and all will be over. So much for the power of Ilestriesa. So much for the humans and their Champion. So much for . . . for . . .

I inhale.

The scent of her hair fills my nostrils—sun-warmed spring grass and, underscoring that, the spicy, unmistakable perfume of *respenia* blossoms.

Suddenly, there it is again. That sense. That . . . that *knowing.* So strong, it's like a fist to the gut, knocking the air from my body.

She's the one.

This frail mortal frame hidden beneath layers of ancient spells she scarcely controls.

She's the one I've waited for. The one I've feared all the long centuries of my life.

Even as my grip firms on my dagger's hilt, I gasp, and it slips from my grasp. My arm trembles around her neck, weakens, and drops away. I fall heavily, crushing her beneath me, then roll to land on my back in the dirt.

I stare into the blue sky at a series of lazy drifting clouds, so far off. The world melts away. A world I'm no longer part of. I'm as far away as those clouds. Floating disembodied above my material husk . . .

Her face swims into view.

I gape at her, not quite comprehending what I see. For a moment, she's the mortal girl, her face flushed as she struggles to reclaim the air I've choked out of her. She blinks down at me through dark lashes, her expression wavering between terror and confusion.

The next moment, Ilestriesa is there, swinging her ax over her head.

Survival instinct flashes through my veins, galvanizing my limbs. I cry out and roll, feeling the reverberation in the ground behind me where the ax chopped into soil instead of my skull. I find my feet and rise, unsteady, sick in my gut. My gaze meets that of the Warrior, and fear surges but . . . but not fear of her . . .

Ilestriesa flies at me. Lunging with her left leg, she

swings her right ax straight up at my jaw. I leap back even as she swoops her left arm down in a whirl of motion mere fractions of an instant before her right ax comes back in play. Her leg slides out to one side, changing the center of her balance as her right arm hacks violently straight down. Only the pulse of living magic in my veins gives me the speed to avoid a devastating blow.

She doesn't stop. The point of her extended ax head aims straight out, leveled at my chest. With a single lunging step, she extends her reach and jabs that point directly into my sternum.

Pain radiates through my chest. I gasp and fall backwards, arms flailing, air driven from my lungs. Ilestriesa is on top of me in an instant, her powerful legs straddling my body, her right arm upraised. The next blow will cleave my chest in two, break through ribs, and expose my heart. I've seen it on the battlefield before. My body will split like old wood before the watching eyes of my people. And the might of Aurelis will go out from the Evenspire, never to be reclaimed.

I see it all in a shining, crystalline instant.

Then *she* is there.

Not Ilestriesa.

The Miphata. The mortal girl.

She stands in that small space of existence inside the Warrior. Un-magicked eyes would never detect her through the glory of the spell, but to my sight she's impossible to miss. Even as Ilestriesa prepares to decimate my body, I cannot take my eyes off the girl.

And she seems to stare straight into my soul.

Ilestriesa's powerful arm moves. The ax blade flashes as it comes whistling down.

The girl's eyes widen.

Her whole body—her very soul—shifts, throws itself against the power indwelling her.

For an instant, everything stills—the Warrior's attack —the clouds drifting overhead—the breath of the onlookers on either side of the field. Everything condenses into a constricted instant in which mere exis- tence is almost unbearable.

Then the ax plunges deep into the ground beside my head.

I gaze up into the Warrior's face bowed close to my own. Ageless. Immobile as stone. Eyes burn like the depths of eternity in a face of carved oblivion.

But that faces melts away, and there she is again. Her features dark, her eyes so blue, framed by puckered dark brows. Her rosebud-shaped lips part with a sharp intake of breath.

In a moment of pure insanity, I wonder what it would be like to touch those lips, to press them against my own.

She steps back. The image of Ilestriesa engulfs her again but wafts in and out of visibility as though the spell struggles to hold on. Then, with a shake of her wild white mane, Ilestriesa yanks herself back into full visibility and takes an aggressive step toward me. Her right-hand ax is still embedded in the dirt, but her left-hand ax lashes out. Before I can even flinch, the blade's edge slides down my cheek, slicing the skin neatly from temple to chin.

Ilestriesa holds aloft her weapon. A line of vivid blue blood drips down its shining silver head.

"I have the blood," she cries out, her words rolling across the field. My people draw back, shrinking away from her like frightened children. *"I have the blood of your king, your champion. The field is mine."*

A murmur of dismay ripples through the air before a mighty cheer from the opposite side of the battleground drowns it out. The humans whoop and hoist their lances, shouting praises to the gods and their Champion. Only then, as their voices beat like drums in my ears, do I realize what has happened.

I've lost.

I live. But I've lost.

The Evenspire belongs to the humans now, by right of the Champion's Blood.

DASYRA

I push back the tent flap, step quickly inside, and let it fall shut behind me. It's a flimsy barrier—merely a curtain of stout canvas between me and the world. But the spells I've put on it muffle the noise outside until it seems to emanate from another realm entirely.

Still, my head rings with the echoes of that ongoing chant: *"Ilestriesa! Ilestriesa! Ilestriesa!"*

The Warrior. The Champion of mortals. Beloved heroine of humankind. Triumphant.

A sob catches in my throat. My trembling hand touches the tender place on my neck where the fae king's arm locked so tight. Choking me . . . not Ilestriesa. *Me. I* felt it. *I* endured it. I suffered the pain and the terror of watching my life shrink down to mere moments, mere heartbeats, as darkness closed in on the edges of my vision. And the Warrior was not there.

How did he do it? How did he pierce through the spell down to the weakness at its core? Down to me?

I grope my way across the tent to the small pile of rugs and bedding in the farthest back corner. There my legs give out, and I sink heavily, barely managing to brace my arms and keep my torso upright. My whole body shakes with aftershock—from both the possession and the terror of the battle itself. It was my first. My first true blood battle. During the two years since the Warrior chose me, I spent most of my time in combat training with the Ualdir Order, under Glarald's tutelage.

But that was different. "Training" as the Vessel didn't involve direct combat on my part. My job was simply to make myself as habitable a host as possible, to not interfere with Ilestriesa while the spirit was upon me.

I interfered today. More than that, I resisted. I threw my soul into battle against Ilestriesa, and . . . and . . .

And I won.

Pressing my hands to my cold cheeks, I bend double over my aching, tension-cramped stomach. Again I relive those terrible moments of battle. The life seeping out of my body as Lodírhal choked me from behind. The weight of him crushing me into the dirt, and that glorious, gasping breath when his grip suddenly loosened, when he released me and collapsed on his back, and I felt the overwhelming power of Ilestriesa fill my spirit and body. Her power then turned upon the fae king, ready to decimate him, to grind him beneath her heel.

And I saw again that look in his eyes. He lay on the ground, gazing up into Ilestriesa's looming face, only he did not see Ilestriesa. He looked deeper.

He looked straight at *me.*

How could I bear to kill a man who looked at me like that?

Mage Jhaan must be furious. And Mage Glarald. They will punish me for what I did, for the mercy I chose. What form their punishment will take, I cannot guess. It will be severe. I know that much. But the rules of the Champion Combat did not specify a need for death. Only blood. And I took his blood, didn't I?

Tears stain my cheeks. I frown, sitting upright again. When did I start crying? Some warrior maiden I am. Ilestriesa certainly never shed a tear after a battle back in the ages lost in history when she walked this world. She probably laughed, quaffed strong drink, and joked with her fellow warriors. She certainly didn't flee to her tent and hide following a victory.

I roughly dash the back of my hand across each cheek, then draw a long breath and hold it, forcing my heartbeat to slow. Jhaan and Glarald will come soon. Just now they're busy seeing to the evacuation of the last of the fae forces—a glorious sight, no doubt. After centuries of occupation, Seryth will be free at last. I ought to be there. I ought to stand at the forefront of my people and watch the flight of my enemy and the dawn of our newfound liberty.

But it isn't *my* liberty. I remain as I've always been: a slave of the Miphates Order. Bound to those powerful figures who dictate my every move, my every thought and deed.

Shaking away a last telltale tear, I bend suddenly and reach under the frame of my bed. My searching hand finds the little box hidden there and pulls it out, setting it in my lap. The interior of my tent is too dark to see much, but I run my fingers lovingly over the delicate lattice carvings decorating the box's lid. Then I flip it open.

A glow fills the small space around me.

Within the box, nestled in soft soil, two little flowers lift bright blue faces, spreading their glittering petals as though to welcome sunlight. One of them shoots out a tendril of green and pulls itself to the edge of the box. I offer my hand, and the tendrils twine around my fingers, lifting the flower right out of the soil. Its pale white roots dangle behind it, wafting gently though there is no breeze.

I lift the flower to my face, touching the soft petals with the tip of my nose, and draw a breath of spicy scent. *Respenia* blossoms—the rarest of all blooms. Grown only in Eledria, the realm of the fae, they are worth entire kingdoms anywhere in this world. These two delicate blossoms have been in my family for several generations, given into my keeping on my sixteenth birthday. A priceless gift.

I lift the respenia bloom to my forehead and feel it climb into my hair, tendrils and roots gripping like dozens of tiny limbs. It nestles happily behind my ear, and I feel the vibration of its contented purr. By this time, the other blossom attempts to climb out as well, its leaves vibrating irritably. It doesn't like to be left behind. "Hold on a moment," I whisper, reaching for it.

The tent flap flings back, admitting a blinding stream of daylight and a cacophony of noise. I start . . . and have just enough presence of mind to slip the second respenia blossom back into the box and snap the lid shut as Jhaan enters, followed swiftly by Glarald.

The two mages blink as their eyes adjust to the dimness of my tent and finally focus on me. I meet their gazes even as I slide the box of soil and its precious occupant under one of my blankets.

"Dark as a tomb in here," Glarald growls and, with a swiftly murmured spell, snaps his fingers. A shining orb sparks into being. He tosses it gently, and it rises to the peak of the tent, there to hover and shed a pale glow over the small space. By its light, Jhaan's white beard appears almost blue, and the frowning crevices outlining his grim mouth deepen.

My old master, leaning on his cane, steps to one side, takes hold of the single chair available, pushes it to the center of the space, and takes a seat directly under the glowing orb. Like a king holding court.

I rise from the bed, my hands clasped tightly at the small of my back, and fight the urge to curtsy. As Vessel of the Warrior, I need not curtsy even to a Miphato of Jhaan's rank.

"Well, Dasyra," he says, his lip curling around my name. Again, he neglects to use my title. "You have disappointed us."

My throat is painfully dry. I try to swallow but can't. "I took first blood," I say, pleased that my voice doesn't tremble as hard as my knees. "I did what I—"

"You interfered with the Warrior." Glarald steps into the space behind Jhaan, one hand gripping the back of the chair. The flash of his teeth in the orb light gives him a feral, dangerous look. "You *know* your role, girl. You are to let the spirit of Ilestriesa flow through you—not bend and manipulate that spirit to your personal whim."

I drop my gaze. Again I try to swallow and fail. Instead, I cough softly.

"What?" Glarald snaps. "Do you have something to say for yourself?"

"Only . . ." I hesitate. But now that I've started, why not continue? "If Ilestriesa is as powerful as you all seem to believe, she wouldn't *let* herself be manipulated. Not against her will."

Glarald seems to swell, his mouth opening, the first inarticulate sounds of an enraged reply garbling in his throat. But Jhaan raises his hand, quieting the younger mage, and fixes me with a level stare, never once blinking.

"Are you implying, child, that the Warrior *wanted* you to take charge? That she deliberately allowed you to alter the results of the battle, to spare King Lodírhal's life?"

It's preposterous. Everyone knows Ilestriesa never hesitates to take what she needs for the sake of her land, her people. She is entirely ruthless. And yet . . .

"I'm merely pointing out what you've always taught me," I answer softly. "Ilestriesa picks her vessels according to her needs. We cannot predict or pretend to understand her purpose with each selection." I lift my chin, meet my master's eyes. "None of you understood her choice when the amulet fell into my keeping. But neither did you doubt her decision. Why should you doubt her now?"

"Because Lodírhal is still alive and breathing," Glarald snarls. He grips the back of Jhaan's chair with both hands as though only just preventing himself from leaping from behind it to throttle me where I stand. "So long as the King of Aurelis lives, we are in danger. Do you imagine he will simply slink back to Eledria with his tail between his legs and never think of the Evenspire again? He will return—a year from now, a decade, a century. It hardly matters which. He will return with a greater force than this world has ever seen. And he will lay waste to all of Seryth as retribution for today's embarrassment."

"I intended no embarrassment. The rules of the Champion Combat state 'to the blood,' not necessarily—"

"Lodírhal doesn't care. A being like that would rather die than live with the shame you caused him. Yet you dared, in your arrogance, to give him shame in place of death. Your *mercy* will cost the lives of thousands."

His words strike like physical blows. I want to flinch, to sit back down on the bed and hide my face. But I can't. I can't let them see how they hurt me. If they knew just how thoroughly I am under their power, where will it stop? They'll go on forever, forcing me into battles, into killings, into being the weapon they need. My life will become one long, blood-soaked horror. Unless I make a stand. Here. Now.

I pull back my shoulders and meet Glarald's gaze. No blinking. No flinching. "I did what I was asked to do. I told you from the beginning that I will not kill. I am *not* Ilestriesa, and I—"

Jhaan stands. Once tall and imposing, now stooped with age, he depends on his cane to support his every step. His bowed head scarcely reaches my shoulder.

But I fear him. Great gods above, I fear him above any other living creature. That calm, quiet potency of his power, far greater, more deep delving than anything Glarald boasts. And that menacing gaze he turns up to me now, craning his neck and twisting his head to one side.

Silently, he approaches. I try to back away but hit the bed frame and sit down hard. He stares into my eyes, now on a level with his—then his gaze shifts. His lashless lids rise, exposing the whites around his dark irises.

In the depths of his pupils, reflected with perfect mirror clarity and glowing in the orb light, is the shining respenia blossom caught in my hair.

Before I can cry out, Jhaan's gnarled hand moves. He catches the little bloom and yanks it free, tearing its roots. Holding it up in the space between us, he looks from it to me and back again.

"You Olorie mages," he hisses. "You and your green things, and your life-growing. You were never meant for true mastery of the *quinsatra*. You were never meant for the glory of a spell like the one you now wear around your neck. But you will learn, child." He smiles then, a kind, paternal sort of smile, steeped in poison. "You will learn to respect the power inside you. You will learn your place among the Miphates."

With a snap of his finger and thumb, he smashes the blossom, grinding stem and leaf and root to a pulp.

I stare. I can't breathe. I can't think. I can only stare . . . and wonder vaguely if my heart stopped beating. If it will ever beat again.

Mage Jhaan drops the remains and pulverizes them

with the stump of his cane, twisting viciously. Then, without so much as a word or a final glance, he turns and totters from the tent.

Glarald remains a moment longer, standing beneath the orb light. He stares fixedly at the smear on the ground and the indentation left behind by the cane. Slowly his gaze rises to meet mine. His face is pale, the rage of a few moments before drained away in shock.

But he shuts his slack jaw tight, spins on one heel, and strides from the tent. The moment the flap falls back into place, the orb light goes out.

I sit in darkness. Alone.

LODÍRHAL

I stand on the deck of a Noxaurian ship, watching the Evenspire fade from sight as we pull out deeper into the Hinter Sea. My people are making for Roseward Isle, which marks the last foothold between this world and the next. There we shall recover for a night or two before continuing to Eledria, putting the human world behind us for good.

My fist clenches, pounding against the rail. Not for good! No, by all the seven gods on high, not for good. I will return to the Dawn Court and gather my strength. I'll amass an army of glorious golden warriors. And trolls. Yes. The trolls of Umbria owe me their allegiance. I'll send them in great warships across the Hinter Sea, set them on the shores of Seryth, and watch as they lay waste to the mortal lands. Let the Miphates hurl their written spells at troll hides! Let them watch their pathetic, bastardized, so-called magic melt into nothing as the ravening hordes tear them apart! The images play out in my head, grim and glorious, a beautiful, bloodthirsty vengeance for the shame I've just suffered.

But all in vain . . . and well I know it.

I flatten my palm on my chest.

Even now, beneath my muddied breastplate, my chainmail, my silken undershirt—beneath flesh and sinew and bone—down in the deeps of my very soul—I feel the curse tightening its hold around my heart.

It's not a true curse. No enemy of mine cast it. It's one of those unpredictable, chance accidents ordained by the gods themselves. Like a disease. The soothsayer present at my christening discovered it, foretelling to all the gathered company the details of my future doom.

"Every strength, she shall weaken," the soothsayer said. *"And every weakness, she shall strengthen, until the balance of power is upended. And your True Name shall be known to her."*

A grimace twists my mouth. I don't remember the soothsayer, having been a mere babe in the cradle at the time the prophecy was spoken. But my mother impressed the words upon me from the time I was old enough to understand. I lived in dread of this day, but . . . well, to be honest, as the centuries slipped away, and with them no sign of any curse, I'd allowed the memory of it to drift into the deeper recesses of my mind.

I wasn't prepared. Not for this.

"Every strength she shall weaken." The words slip bitterly from my lips as I watch the haze of distance overwhelm the Evenspire. Already, the first part of the curse has come to pass—I've lost. The power of Aurelis, once uncontested, is gone from the human world. And here I am, fleeing like a cur with its tail between its legs. Beaten in battle before the eyes of all my people.

That girl, that mortal creature—she may be my Fated Love, but in this moment I could not hate anyone more.

"That, great king, was one of the most disastrous sights I've ever had the pleasure of witnessing."

The sound of that smooth, dark, maliciously cheerful voice makes the skin on the back of my neck crawl. Assuming a mask of imperturbable calm, I turn from the rail to face Kyriakos, Lord of Ninthalor. My longtime friend, sometime enemy regards me with eyes the black of deepest night. His complexion is the dusky gray, almost lavender of a Noxaur fae, and seems out of place here under the light of midday sun.

I've known him all my life. We played together as boys, fought as youths, and over the centuries developed a mutual respect and distrust. I've always admired his ruthlessness. Kyriakos never hesitates to do whatever is required to accomplish his ends. He is not a king . . . but he has all the makings of one, including the ambition to claim a crown for himself. Thus King Beldroth of Noxaur takes pains to send his mightiest lord on missions to the farthest reaches of Eledria and the worlds beyond whenever possible.

Kyriakos approaches the rail and leans against it, his height equal to mine. The sea wind snaps his dark hair across his face like a veil that fails to disguise the malignant pleasure in his expression. "I won't lie: For a moment there I thought you would carry the day. It seemed to all of us that you had the mortal magess well in hand. But alas! It seems your gentler nature got the best of you in the end." He tosses me a careless grin. "What was it, Lodírhal? Couldn't bear to kill a female with your bare hands?"

Choosing to ignore the bait, I look back to the sea and the disappearing horizon. I let the silence linger between us a little longer than is altogether comfortable before finally growling, "You took your time answering the summons." It's not exactly an accusation. More of a statement.

Kyriakos turns around and rests his elbows on the rail, leaning far back and lifting his face to the sky above. "I was well on my way, believe you me . . . but then I caught a whiff of an intriguing perfume off the coast of Hagmar. A young human witch. Utterly delectable thing. Wooing her took some time, but ah! T'was worth it in the end. She has tremendous power for so slight a creature."

"Another prize for your growing harem?" I ask with a sneer.

Kyriakos raises an eyebrow, catching my disapproving gaze. "If I'm not much mistaken, the child even now growing in her belly will be a powerful Hybrid-magic user. Perhaps even a match for that mortal magess who just wiped the field with your pretty face."

I shudder and look away again before I say something I'll regret. But Kyriakos reads my expression and laughs outright. "Come, my friend. You lost the battle. Hells, you even lost the war. But there will be more wars. There are always more wars. Let the mortals enjoy their victory for a handful of decades. Let them think they've won. You will rally again and return in due time."

Would that he spoke the truth! I touch my breastplate

again, that place just over my heart. Even as I do so, the final tip of the Evenspire fades fully from view and I . . .

I suck in a tight breath and grasp the rail in front of me. Something is wrong. Something radiates from my heart out through my limbs: a coldness. Unbearable coldness, freezing my blood. My knees quake, and I sag where I stand.

"Lodírhal?" Kyriakos's voice loses some of its flippant triumph. "Lodírhal, what is this—"

I lose the rest of his question as a fresh wave of cold crashes over me, knocking me flat on my back. I stare at the snapping black sails overhead, but my gaze swims, darkens. Distantly I feel the shock shaking my body, causing me to thrash beyond control. Someone speaks my name. Someone is calling for help. Someone bows over me and then . . . and then . . .

I wake in a cabin, sprawled on a narrow berth. Enbalar is there, hovering over me, his ugly, battle-torn face made even uglier with fear. Behind him, Kyriakos stands in shadows, his dark eyes glinting in the light falling through one of the narrow windows.

"My king?" Enbalar says, his hands gripping my shoulders. Stripped of breastplate and mail, I'm clad only in my undershirt. "My king, can you hear me?"

I try to speak, but my tongue feels thick and wooden. I nod instead and manage a small groan that brings a momentary wash of relief across my seneschal's face. But then he bares his teeth.

"It's a curse," he growls. "Ilestriesa must have cursed you when she cut your cheek, and now it's working its way into you. So much for her show of mercy! We should turn this ship around, summon the others. We should storm the shores and show them—"

Kyriakos interrupts with a bark of laughter and plants his heavy hand on my seneschal's shoulder. "Your king needs a drink, I believe. Why don't you fetch it for him?"

Enbalar shakes off Kyriakos's grip. "Summon a servant," he snarls. But Kyriakos fixes him with a look of deadly intent. Enbalar, though a brave man and renowned warrior, blenches. He glances at me again, his jaw twisting with frustration. Then, with a bow, he exits the crowded cabin, leaving me alone with the Lord of Ninthalor.

Kyriakos takes a seat on a richly upholstered chair, leaning back and crossing his arms. He props one foot on the end of the bunk, though there is scarcely room enough for me as it is. His head tilting to one side, he fixes me with a narrow-eyed stare.

"This isn't a curse. Is it?"

I shake my head. "Not exactly." Shifting my hands beneath me, I try to rise. A wave of sickness overwhelms me, shivering like ice through my limbs. I fight it, refusing to lie back down, and succeed for the moment. But it will get worse. The greater the distance grows between me and that girl . . .

Kyriakos offers no assistance as I struggle upright and swing my legs over the edge of the berth. He merely asks, "What are you going to do about it?"

I glance up, catch his eye, and see that he has guessed the truth. Or at least come much closer to it than Enbalar.

My mouth opens, but I don't know how to answer. We

41

are both familiar with the gods-ordained Law of the Fate-bound. Incidents of it seldom occur . . . but when they do, its effects are obvious. And inescapable.

That mage girl is my Fated Love. I must take her to wife. Not merely to bed, but truly to wife, with all the sacred vows spoken to Nornala, goddess of unity. I must leave and cleave only to her for the rest of our designated days. And if I do not . . .

I feel the weakness permeating my blood, sense the chill as my magic slowly dies in my veins. If I fail to honor the sacred bonds of this gods-decreed love, I will lose all my power, all my magic. Then I will die.

She shall weaken every strength . . .

I feel Kyriakos watching me closely. Gods above, I must not show weakness before him. But when I start to rise from the berth, the whole world pitches around me as though we've suddenly entered a storm. My stomach churns, and the coldness in my body makes me tremble so hard, I start to fall.

Kyriakos catches my shoulders and holds me upright. "So, this is why you didn't kill her," he says, his voice a low rumble. "To kill your Fatebonded is to kill yourself. What an unfortunate turn of events." He chuckles as he assists me back onto the berth. "No matter, great king. There's always a way out of even the tightest snare."

"A way out?" Though I hate myself for it, I look up, hope sparking in my breast. I shouldn't let Kyriakos play me like this. But I can't help myself. "What do you know?"

"Not much, admittedly. But about Fatebinding? More than you might think."

"Go on." I refuse to add the unspoken *please,* but it's there in my voice.

Kyriakos smiles. "Oh, my dear Lodírhal! You can't get something for nothing, you know. If I tell you the way to break this binding, I need something in return. Something worth the price."

Bile roils in my gut, yet I can't argue. This is the way of Eledria, after all. Bargains struck; deals made. Never give without receiving.

"Name your price, Kyriakos."

The lord of Ninthalor leans closer, his sharp teeth flashing in a tiger's smile. "Ilestriesa," he says. "I want the amulet. I want the power of the Incarnate Warrior."

So this is his game. It shouldn't surprise me. He always was one to angle an advantage to increase his strength.

"I don't believe I can get the amulet for you," I say, choosing my words with care. "Not without killing the Vessel. And, as you've stated, I cannot kill her without killing myself."

"Ah, but that is not necessarily true." Kyriakos reclaims his chair and leans back comfortably. "If you succeed in the little mission I have for you, you will certainly kill her. And her amulet will fall into your hands. What I want is your word that, should you succeed, you will turn that amulet . . . turn Ilestriesa . . . over to me."

I stare into his impenetrable dark eyes. What would it mean to deliver such a power into Kyriakos's ferocious grasp? He could never wield the Warrior spell himself. But he has human wives, a great collection of them, all endowed with magic—witches and mages and lovely girls untrained but possessed of the spark. Surely one of them would prove a worthy Vessel. And then what havoc might Kyriakos unleash upon Eledria? Upon the worlds?

No. I can't be responsible. I can't—

Another wave of sickness crashes into me, and I collapse onto the bed, my limbs shaking beyond control. Darkness closes in, and I am lost to the pain for I don't know how long. I feel magic seep out through my pores, and my soul somehow perceives it rising like a miasma around me.

When I regain consciousness, Kyriakos stands at the window, gazing out at the sea. Though he does not look around, he is aware of my return to consciousness. "We have reached the shores of Roseward," he says, slowly turning to meet my haggard gaze. "You will not survive beyond this point, great king. Should you attempt to venture past Roseward without your Fatebonded at your side, you will surely die."

In three long strides he returns to the bedside to bow over me, his teeth bared in an awful smile. "Make the bargain with me, Lodírhal. If you succeed in breaking the Fatebond, Ilestriesa is mine. Say it. Say it."

I want to resist. But what choice do I have? If I die, I leave no heir. The kingdom of Aurelis would be thrown into turmoil, particularly following this great defeat in the human world. I cannot do that to my people. I am more than just myself.

I open my cracked lips and croak out the words: "By Ralocan Lodírhal—the True Name of my gods-rested father—I vow: Should I succeed in breaking the Fate-bond, Ilestriesa's amulet is yours."

Another surge of pain rips through my body, making me gasp and flail. When one of my wildly lashing arms lands in Kyriakos's strong grasp, I stare up at him.

"Tell me," I beg. "Tell me how to save myself."

DASYRA

I force myself to wait until nightfall. And then I wait another four hours, until the night is very deep indeed.

Through the shielding spells on my tent, I can just discern sounds of revelry, which have replaced the sounds of activity and movement and purpose from earlier in the day. The fae have gone from Seryth's shores . . . and now the army of Seryth gives way to pure celebration. Not even Mage Jhaan could stop them, for all his stern demeanor and commanding presence. The entire encampment will be drunk and delirious on victory and wine. Glarald and most of the other Miphates will be right there in their midst.

This is my chance. My only chance.

I wrap a fur-lined cloak tightly around my shoulders. As I fasten the clasp at my throat, I pause a moment and touch the amulet tucked beneath my gown's bodice. If only I could tear it off and fling it to the dirt! Grind it beneath my heel the way Jhaan ground my respenia bloom. But I can't. Ilestriesa chose me. I'm bound to the Warrior Spirit. I might yank the amulet, break its chain, and hurl it as hard as I can from the highest cliff into the sea . . . but before I turned away and walked three paces, it would be back around my neck again. A shackle I must bear to the end of my life.

My jaw firms. I might be bound to their Warrior. But that doesn't mean I will remain bound to the Miphates.

Perching on the edge of my bed, I slip the delicate carved box from its hiding place under the blanket. I open it, peer inside . . . and my heart threatens to break. The blossom is faded. Its bright blue petals are pale, almost colorless. It lifts its face to me, and for a moment I see a little flare of color shoot out from its yellow center. But the effort is too great, and the bloom shrinks again, pulling into itself, closing its petals tight.

"I'm so sorry," I breathe. "I'm so very sorry."

I rest my hand in the box, my fingers close to the bloom. For a moment it doesn't move. Then, to my relief, it extends a tentative tendril and wraps around my index finger. When I lift, it relinquishes its hold on the dirt, allowing me to draw it up from the box. I tuck it into my hair, feel it arranging itself above my ear in the same place where the now dead blossom had perched. After a moment, it begins to purr faintly.

Respenia always come in pairs. It's a well-known fact. A fact with which Mage Jhaan was certainly familiar, gods blight him. Now that this one's mate is gone . . . how much longer will it live?

I quickly blink tears from my blurring eyes. This is no time to dissolve into weeping. I must do what I can for the little bloom. A ward witch lives in Hagmar County, not far from here. She might know a way into Eledria. Perhaps I can venture through and find a new respenia blossom before this one wilts and dies.

Lifting my chin in resolution, I stride across the tent, and stand before the tent flap. Despite the heat of blood pulsing in my veins, I pause. My breath tightens. Am I really doing this? I've been a student of the Miphates Order since I was ten years old. Can I bear to break those bonds, to flee this service to which I've dedicated my life?

And if they catch me . . . if they hunt me down and drag me back . . . what will they do to me then?

Fingers trembling, I touch the respenia behind my ear. It shivers, then leans into my touch, desperate for comfort. That little brush of petals gives me strength. I can do this. I *must* do this. Vessel or no vessel, I am first and foremost an Olorie Mage, dedicated to the growing and nurturing of all living things. I'll save this blossom if it's the last thing I do.

I sweep back the tent flap. And stare.

Someone is there. Standing in front of me. Someone I cannot quite see, backlit as he is by the reveling army's bonfires. Someone very tall, broad. Someone . . . not human.

"Who are you?" I gasp, drawing a step back into the tent.

He follows me, closing the distance between us. For an instant—less than a single heartbeat of a moment—I see through the darkening glamour he wears to a pair of brilliant gold eyes shining in an exquisitely beautiful face.

"You!" I gasp.

Then darkness overwhelms me, like the sweep of a cloak obscuring my sight. I fight against it, thrash, try to resist. My hand reaches for my amulet, and my tongue tries to form the words of the summoning spell. But it's already too late.

The last thing I recall before succumbing to unconsciousness is a pair of strong arms catching me as I collapse.

LODÍRHAL

The humans are lost to their revels, delirious with joy at the humiliation of my people. I hate them with a passion that burns like poison in my gut. Yet for the moment, I must be grateful that they are far too drunk on both wine and victory to take note of me and my shielding glamour as I slip through their midst, bearing the limp body of the Vessel over my shoulder.

My strength has returned. The moment I stepped back onto Serythian soil, the moment I approached this girl, I felt it rushing back like a river suddenly undammed. I'm stronger than I've been in years, since before we lost the spires. Not even the strongest of their Miphates could break through my illusions now.

Thus I carry the young magess out from the camp uncontested and make my way down to the coast where I've hidden a small sailing craft. It too is shrouded in spells to shield it from any vigilant eyes, but no watch is set on the shores of Seryth tonight. Their enemy has retreated. For good, they believe.

I shall return. I swear it.

I simply must deal with this little ... *problem* first.

I bundle the human girl into the bow of the boat, trying not to hurt her in my haste. Although I care nothing for her ultimate health and happiness, for as long as the Fatebond remains, any hurt I cause her brings equal or greater pain to myself. I need to be wary.

Pushing the boat out into deeper water, I climb aboard, adjust its sails to catch the night breeze, and set out along the coastline. I cannot return to Roseward, not with the Miphata in hand. There would be far too many questions. Rumors would spread, and word would swiftly reach my enemies. I am vulnerable now as I have never been before.

She shall weaken every strength ...

Truer words were never spoken.

The sea is easy tonight, the winds gentle, the currents calm. I make good progress along the coastline. Like all people of the Dawn Court, I do not love the dark, but there is plenty of moonlight to aid me. I concentrate on the angle of my sails and the balance of my craft and try not to let my gaze return to the sleeping Miphata. Only .. . only ...

Only, gods help me, it's more difficult than I imagined. I feel ... *thirsty* for her. Parched and desperate for a glimpse of her face. And every time I give in, every time I surrender to the yearning, I am struck to the heart. She's so beautiful.

Except, of course, she's not. She's only a human. I've been surrounded by far more beautiful women all my life, can take my pick of them. This girl is nothing by comparison, base and mortal and dirt bound as she is, with no trace of natural magic flowing in her veins.

But something about the delicate imperfection of her features is intriguing. The slightly crooked set of her nose. The faded scar just above her eyebrow. All those lovely little testimonies to her lack of glamour. She is authentically herself, without adornment. Who would have believed that all those assorted flaws, when brought together, could form such a beautiful whole?

It has to be the Fatebond manipulating my eyes, warping my reason. Making me see what isn't there. Gods spare me! The sooner I break this bond the better.

Kyriakos's words echo in the back of my head: *"If you have the will—if you have the strength—to do what must be done."*

I have the will. And I am stronger than any weakness this girl may awaken in me.

I hear a moan from the bow and brace myself. She's stirring. She isn't going to be happy. As I watch, the young magess's eyes flutter and suddenly flare wide. A scream chokes in her throat as she sits upright, grabs hold of the gunwale with her bound hands, and stares around, her jolting motions rocking the boat. Her next scream emerges as a gurgling mewl.

"You would do well to calm yourself, Miphata, lest you capsize our craft," I say, my voice pitched low. "We are far from shore, and your heavy skirts will surely drag you to the bottom of the ocean. A pitiful end."

At the sound of my voice, she whirls to face me, nearly falling off her small bench seat. Only her grip on the gunwale keeps her upright. Her eyes, white-ringed in the moonlight, flick from me down to her hands, which she twists, trying to free herself. But those cords are woven from a basilisk's bristles. They won't give or break.

She abruptly stops struggling and lifts her hands to her chest, desperately feeling around. Her gaze flashes back to meet mine.

"Looking for this?" I ask. Reaching into the front of my doublet, I withdraw the amulet and hold it up.

Her mouth drops slowly open. "How . . . how did you do that?"

Hardly the question I would have expected from her in that moment. "Do what?" I ask.

"Take my amulet!" She shakes her head, her face a mask of horror and shock. "No one can take it from me!"

I raise an eyebrow and tuck the ensorcelled talisman back inside my doublet. "Apparently you've been misled in that belief, Miphata."

Her dark hair has pulled free of its ribbons and falls about her pale face. Her gaze fixes on my breast with uncomfortable intensity, and I shift slightly in my seat, careful not to jostle the tiller. Silence extends between us. At last, she tears her gaze away and scans the coast, half a mile off to her right. "Where . . . where are you taking me?" she asks, turning those horribly compelling eyes of hers back to me.

"To Hagmar," I answer simply.

She blinks, her mouth opening and closing three times. Finally, she manages, "Wh-why?"

"I believe there is a gate there. A way into the Hinter Paths that is, as yet, unbroken by your Miphates brothers."

"Are you . . . are you taking me to Eledria?"

"Yes."

Again, she stares unspeaking for some moments before blurting, "Why?"

Although I don't want to answer, I can't accomplish my mission without informing her of the situation. Still, I can't very well say, *Turns out, you're my Fated Bride unless we do something about it.* She won't believe me. I must convince her. Somehow.

And she shall know your True Name.

The soothsayer's words echo like doom inside my head. I narrow my eyes. But maybe there is a way . . .

"Tell me, Miphata," I say sharply, "do you know my True Name?"

She looks confused. "I . . . No. Of course not." Her brow puckers, and she turns her head a little to one side to study me. "I know you are King Lodírhal of Aurelis. That's all."

Good. The Fatebond hasn't given her *that* power over me, at least. Not yet. Still, I must push for more.

"Try," I say. "Reach down inside yourself and see if you can sense . . . sense a connection. Like a thread strung between us."

"You're mad."

I almost snort. "Perhaps. Try anyway."

She shoots me a shrewd glance. Then, to my surprise, she closes her eyes, and I watch her body begin to relax there on the bench. She sinks quickly and naturally into a trancelike state. She's good at this. Good at stilling her mind, at reaching down through the upper levels of consciousness into the deeper recesses of the soul. I feel a grudging respect.

Suddenly, I gasp. Something in the air between us sparks with life, with fire. For a brief, agonizing moment, I can almost see it shining in the air, bright as a filament of flame. The girl utters a little cry. The brilliance vanishes into the ether, and I find myself staring across the small craft into her blinking eyes.

"I . . . I almost did it," she says, her voice trembling with wonder and fear. "Your name . . . I could almost . . . I thought I could . . ." With her bound hands she pushes sea-swept hair from her eyes. "How did you do that? How and . . . and *why?*"

She understands the danger to me in having my True Name to be known. She's familiar with the ways of my people.

"*I* am not doing it," I answer coldly. "It is the result of a power much greater and older than mine, a power said to stem from the gods themselves—the Fatebond."

Her face is blank, uncomprehending.

"Have you heard of it?"

She shakes her head slowly. Gods blight it! I'd hoped she would understand without explanations.

"It would seem, Miphata," I say, meeting her gaze levelly, "that you and I have been predestined before the beginning of time to be each other's True Love. *Yllamiryl*, as we say in my tongue. Fatebonded. At the moment of our first meeting, our souls became inextricably tied to one another, and only death may separate us."

She gapes at me. I watch the slow horror dawning in

her eyes. She opens her mouth, but no words come. Finally, she says softly, "Now I know you're mad."

"Unfortunately, I am not. Madness would certainly be preferable. This binding is so absolute that we must wed or die."

"So, you . . ." She stops, swallows hard, and shifts backward in her seat. "You've kidnapped me to *marry* me?"

Despite myself, a smile curves the corner of my mouth. Her horror is absolute—yet not one fae maid in all the Dawn Court wouldn't love to stand in her shoes. Still, I can't be offended since her feeling is amply reciprocated.

"I rather hope *not*," I say. "Indeed, the last thing I wish is to find myself bound to a human for life. Particularly a Miphata."

Her lip curls. "Particularly a Miphata who just trounced you in front of your people?"

If only I could strike her for this insolence! No human should dare speak to me thus. But I restrain my hand and my tongue, answering only, "As luck would have it, our cause is not utterly without hope. I have been told of a way to sever our Fatebond. But it requires a journey. You and I must travel together to the Sundering Place."

"The Sundering Place?" She lifts her chin slightly. "Where is that?"

"I don't know. No one knows for certain."

Once again she gapes at me, her delicate rosebud lips parted. "So how are we supposed to get there? To break this bond?"

"We must ask a magic user from among your own people to tell us the way."

"But . . . but how is that supposed to work if no one *knows* the way?"

I sigh. Any fae child would know the answer to this. But then, she did not grow up in Eledria. I cannot fault her for being unfamiliar with its ways. "The one we ask need not *know* the way. They must only *decide* the way, and the Paths of the Hinter will shape themselves accordingly."

Her mouth opens to question me further, then shuts. After considering briefly, she nods, apparently accepting my explanation. She's a sharp one. I'll give her that.

"Why are we going to Hagmar then?" she asks after a bit. "I am a magic user. Can I not decide for us?"

"Unfortunately not, as you are one of the Fatebonded in this instance."

"But we just left behind a whole camp full of Miphates. Couldn't we have asked . . . well, no." She stops herself, shrugging and pinching her lips together. "I suppose they would have panicked to find you back in their camp. They certainly wouldn't stop to listen to all this Fatebinding nonsense before blasting you with spells."

"My reasoning exactly."

She shoots me another shrewd look. "There's a ward witch in Hagmar."

"I know. Thus, to Hagmar we go. And we will ask the witch to determine our way to the Sundering Place. Then we'll make the journey and, should we survive, we'll break the Fatebond and be free."

"And be free," she echoes softly. As her gaze slips away from mine again, out to the open sea, her eyes hold an expression I don't quite understand. Longing? I watch her hands rise to her bosom, to the place between her breasts. Strange . . . she has not yet suggested exchanging Ilestriesa's amulet for her compliance on this journey. She seems singularly uninterested in the return of her power.

Finally, she turns and looks me straight in the eye. "Very well, Lodírhal of Aurelis. I will journey with you to this Sundering Place." She offers a small, rueful smile. "Let us end whatever connection exists between us once and for all."

With these words, she slips from the bench and kneels before me, holding out her hands. I hesitate, uncertain what she wants. Then, slowly, I extend my hands and grip hers, sealing our agreement.

A mistake.

The instant my skin contacts hers, something surges through me. Something painful and . . . and glorious. I feel both empowered and undone, as though I could leap as high as the heavens, only to fall broken at her feet.

I stare at her fingers, small and dark in mine, and fight the urge to raise them to my lips. Desperately I tear my gaze away, but this is a mistake as well. For now I'm captured by her lips. Soft and gently parted. Like petals of a flower whose nectar waits to be sipped.

Over the long centuries of my existence I've kissed hundreds of beautiful women. . . but for the second time I find myself wondering what it would be like be to kiss *her*.

My eyes widen. With a sharp intake of breath, I drop her hands and sit back in my seat, my face fixed in hard lines. Did she feel it? Did she sense the weakness in me? I must be cautious. How can I survive the journey ahead of us if I am so easily unmanned in her presence?

She rises, a little awkward as she settles back on her seat across from me, leaning her elbows on her knees. After a few silent minutes, she asks, "So, are you going to untie me or what?"

DASYRA

I suppose, when all's said and done, this is convenient.

I mean, I was already planning to run away to Hagmar, wasn't I? Planning to ask the ward witch there the way into Eledria. Planning to put as much distance between myself and Mage Jhaan and Mage Glarald as I possibly could.

So, if King Lodírhal of all people wants to help me out with these first few legs of the journey, why kick up a fuss? I'm not saying I believe all this nonsense about fate and the gods. Perhaps it makes a sort of sense . . . after all, why else would he kidnap me like this, spiriting me away in the middle of the night?

Unless his ultimate goal is to claim Ilestriesa.

My hand, newly freed of its binding, touches empty space beneath my bodice where the amulet should rest. I never thought I'd live to see the day when I was free of its weight that had, in the last two years, become as familiar a part of me as my own right arm. The spell-vows of the Vessel should have prevented separation at any cost short of my death. And yet, impossibly, this golden-eyed fae king, my enemy, took it from me as if it were a mere trinket.

Well, let him have it. Gods on high, I would give just about anything to be rid of that burden! To be free . . .

I glance at my captor seated at the tiller, his gaze following the coastline. Moonlight illuminates the planes of his cheeks and brow, glints bright in the dark pupils of his eyes. A sea breeze tosses his hair behind him, pale and silvery in that light, though I know it to be of richest, sun-kissed gold.

Could I truly be—what was the word he used?—*Fate-bound* to such a man? Such a being? Just looking at him, swathed in glamours as he is, makes me feel so base and dirty. So foolish and simple and small. Certainly not how I'd wish to feel in the presence of a potential mate.

My hand rises from my chest to my throat, where I can still almost feel the pressure of his arm choking the air out of me. Granted, our battle was honorable, fought for the purpose of saving many lives, but still . . . I shudder.

"There." The king's voice startles me out of my reverie. He raises one arm to point at the coast. I turn, straining my vision. Is that the coast of Hagmar? I've never seen it from the sea, so I can't say for certain. I do spy a lone cottage on a hillside above a stretch of beach.

"I sense something," Lodírhal says. After a moment he grunts and adds, "Kyriakos was right: That is a potent magical aura. This witch must possess a strong gift."

I narrow my eyes. The cottage is still much too far

away for me to get any magical reading off it even if I tried. But then, the fae are in tune with the forces of the *quinsatra* in ways even the strongest Miphates cannot mimic.

Lodírhal guides his small vessel toward the beach, his every motion confident and precise, as though he were a born seafarer. I crouch in the prow, taking care to stay out of the way of the shifting sail. My stomach churns uneasily; I look forward to having dry ground under my feet again. The small craft's prow nestles into the shore, its wooden hull crunching against sand and stone. Careful to avoid the sail, I spring out, yelping as my feet sink into freezing water up to my calves.

Behind me, Lodírhal's voice barks, *"Stop."*

The single word is like an arrow to my spine. For an instant I freeze in place . . . but the instant passes, and I stagger several paces through the surf and foam. Shaking my head and shoulders, I turn and scowl at the fae king, who watches me wide-eyed.

Did he just try to use a spell on me? I think so. Apparently, this Fatebond of ours makes me resistant to his magic. Something he hadn't anticipated, by the look on his moon-washed face.

I grab the boat and try to haul it further onto the shore. Lodírhal joins me, catching hold of the gunwale and moving with such strength and ease that the boat fairly glides up onto the sand. Only when he's certain it's secure does he look at me again.

I cast him a wry grin and cross my arms. "What? Did you think I was going to run for it?"

His lip curls. He turns without answer and heads up

the beach toward that cottage on the rise. I lift my sodden skirts and hurry after him, momentarily relieved to leave the cold water behind. But my relief is short-lived as the beach's rough stones tear through the soles of my slippers. I stagger, yelp, and start to fall.

A strong hand grasps my elbow. "Careful."

I look up.

Something about the way he said that word . . . softly, gently . . . a little husky with concern . . . was more shocking than the barked spell he'd flung at my back. For a moment, I catch his eye. And find it suddenly difficult to breathe.

"I'm all right." I straighten and shake my arm roughly, pulling free. The sharpness of my gesture is almost enough to send me tumbling again, but I catch my balance and draw myself upright. "Let's go."

He takes a step back, then another, still staring at me. Why does he look at me that way?

Before I can begin to fathom an answer, he turns and heads on up the beach, his cloak billowing behind him like a pair of white wings in the night. I breathe out a little huff of air and push hair from my face. As I do, my finger brushes the petals of the respenia blossom tucked behind my ear. It shivers at my touch, and I feel the vibration of its purr, weak but still present.

"Don't worry, little one," I whisper. "I will help you. I promise. Fae king or no fae king."

The walk to the cottage door is longer than it looked, and my skirts are so heavy with seawater and accumulated sand that I must hike them halfway up my calves to walk. My wardrobe is certainly ill planned for adventuring. Ilestriesa would laugh if she could see her hapless Vessel now. Good thing she's safely in Lodírhal's keeping.

I keep one eye on my captor's moonlit head, the other on my feet, taking care not to trip in the darkness and trying to stop myself from looking ahead and willing the cottage to move closer. Suddenly, the night is washed in a warm yellow glow. Startled, I look up to see the cottage now a mere five yards further up the slope. In its open doorway, firelight silhouettes a thickset figure wielding a rune-staff fulgent with accumulated spell-light. Its blazing tip points directly at Lodírhal's chest.

"Wait!" I leap forward to stand between the fae king and the ward witch. Beyond the glow, I see the witch's face highlighted in sharp relief. She's young, I notice with surprise. No more than a few years older than me, and pretty in a ruddy, sea-swept sort of way. Her eyes narrow into a ferocious glare as she stares me down over the length of her staff.

"You ain't a fae," she growls.

"No, indeed." I wave my hands as though to emphasize my words. "I am Mage Rolim of the Miphates. We're here to ask—"

"But you dare bring a fae to my doorstep?" The witch turns her head to one side and spits loudly, her pretty mouth curling into an ugly shape. "Traitor!" She adjusts the angle of her staff, and the spell again begins to amplify. My mouth drops open as I gape into that mounting power, frozen as though hypnotized.

A sweep of cloak flashes before my vision, and I'm suddenly behind King Lodírhal, gazing at the witch from around his broad shoulders. His voice rings clearly in the night. "Mother Erlani."

Mother? That witch is far too young to have earned the title "Mother," which is eventually granted to most ward witches regardless of maternal status. At her age she ought still to be called *Mistress* Erlani, oughtn't she?

But then the young witch's hands begin to shake. The end of her staff drops to one side, and as the red glow of her spell recedes, I notice for the first time that she isn't simply plump—she is positively rotund. Heavy with child. She stares at Lodírhal, her wide eyes gleaming in the moonlight. "How . . . how do you know my name?"

"It was given to me," Lodírhal replies, "by Kyriakos, Lord of Ninthalor. It was he who told me to seek you out and request your aid."

The witch swallows, her gaze flicking from the fae king to me and back again. One hand uneasily strokes her swelling stomach.

Kyriakos . . . That's a fae name. One I may even have heard before. Did the young ward witch truly give her name to a fae despite her apparent hatred of them? Or had this Kyriakos tricked it out of her? Regardless, the witch turns her staff with her fingers and sets her chin. Her puckered brow smooths into a stern mask.

"Fine," she says. "Speak, fae. Tell me what you need."

I hear Lodírhal quietly release a held breath. Apparently, this small woman and her power intimidate even him. "I seek the road to the Sundering Place," he says. "I am told you may tell me the way."

The witch narrows her eyes again. The silence lasts so long, I begin to wonder if she doesn't understand. After all, I never heard of either Fatebindings or the Sundering Place until tonight, and I was brought up as a Miphata, right in the center of all magical learning. Could a ward witch have learned more of the ways of Faerieland than I? Surely not out here in this remote part of nowhere. I open my mouth, prepared to offer an explanation.

Before the words leave my mouth, however, the witch begins to speak: "The way you seek . . . for you it must be thus: Together, you and your Bonded will travel seven days and seven nights. You will face seven perils, and you will survive together or not at all. Thus will you reach the Sundering Place."

Lodírhal utters a word I don't know. From the sound of it, I'd guess it's a curse. I can't blame him. Seven days and seven nights? Traveling with this man? I suspect the witch is being spiteful, forcing us together for much longer than she needs to. Still, if it means I'm free at the end of it . . . free of him, free of Mage Jhaan, free of the Miphates . . .

"Very well, witch," Lodírhal snarls. "Tell me where to begin this journey and what my route must be."

The young witch smiles. "Your journey must begin at the Gate of Wyndithas. You will cross over into the Goran Desolation and journey across that wide waste. Should you survive, you will face the guardian of the Bridge of Caibalar. . ."

She continues in this vein for some time, spinning out a series of names and places that mean absolutely nothing to me. This ward witch is apparently far more familiar with the ways of the worlds than I am, isolated little Olorie student that I've been. I glance from her to

Lodírhal and can see by the tension tightening in his cheek—and the way he carefully tries to hide it—that *he*, at least, is familiar with all these names. And none of them are good.

The witch at last draws to a close, saying, "In this way and this alone will you reach the Sundering Place. There may the judgement of the gods fall upon you both."

This seems to be the end of it. I'm not sure if thanks are in order. Lodírhal certainly doesn't look grateful. He stands for a long moment, refusing to break eye contact with the witch. Then, with a flash of snarling teeth, he turns on his heel and sets off striding into the night. Not back toward the beach and the boat, I notice.

I gape after him, momentarily undecided. I should follow, of course. I've agreed to make this journey—need to make it, apparently, for my own sake as much as his. But . . .

Acting on impulse, I turn and spring a few steps closer to the ward witch. "Wait, please," I call out just as she starts to shut her door.

The witch pauses and peers out at me. "I'm sorry," she says, some of the anger melting from her voice. "I know I've made this tough on you. But if my choices tonight mean a chance to end the life of one of these wretches—"

"No, I don't care about any of that," I say, waving a hand. Lodírhal will notice I'm not with him in a moment and return for me. I must ask my question while I can. "I just want to know . . . can you tell me where respenia blossoms grow?"

"Respenia?" The witch opens her door a little wider, her brow furrowing as she gives me a stern look. Her gaze flicks from me to Lodírhal's retreating figure, nearly vanished into the darkness. "Why?"

"I just . . . I need to know."

She shakes her head slowly. "You're a mage, ain't you?"

"Yes."

"A Miphata of the Olorie Order?"

I nod.

"Take my advice then, Olorie. Don't worry yourself about all your little green and growing things. Worry about that monster you're bound to. Get yourself unbound and free before . . . before . . ." She bites her lip. One hand runs slowly along the swell of her belly, and her face momentarily softens into an expression I cannot name. "Before you find you don't want to be free anymore."

With that, she steps back into her cottage and shuts the door.

LODÍRHAL

"So where exactly are we going?"

The young Miphata's voice tugs at my ear, drawing me out of the darkness of my thoughts. I look over my shoulder to glare down at her. "To the Gate of Wyndithas." The words spit bitterly from my tongue. "Just as the witch declared."

Though I face forward to avoid looking at her any more than I must, she trots up alongside me. I feel her gaze burn into the side of my face. "I'm guessing this turn of events isn't quite what you'd hoped," she says dryly, waving one hand in a circular gesture. "I mean, your sunny demeanor has all but vanished."

I shoot another glare down at her. Is she laughing at me? No one laughs at me! My lips pull back, and I prepare to snarl a response, to put her in her place. But then she smiles, and it's so bright, so disarming . . . I lose all words.

I realize I've stopped walking. And I'm still staring.

"Come on," she says, tilting her head to one side. "Out

with it: What's so bad about this gate? It'll get us into Eledria, right?"

With a quick shake of my head, I clear my throat and draw my brows down into a knot. "It will." My answer is abrupt, stern . . . and edged with a traitorous tremble. "But it's a perilous gate. And even should we survive the passing, we will emerge in the Goran Desolation."

"I'm guessing with a name like that, it isn't a favorite picnic ground."

I raise an eyebrow. How can she be so cavalier about this? But then, she is unfamiliar with Eledria and its ways. Gods above, it will be more complicated than I thought, getting her to the Sundering Place in one piece. That ward witch certainly did her best to hamstring me.

But was it her doing? Or was she merely Kyriakos's puppet?

The young Miphata still awaits my answer.

"The Goran Desolation," I say, "is a land of Wild Magic. The veil of the *quinsatra* is too thin there, and pure magic seeps through and permeates the land, the flora, the fauna. Warps it in utterly unpredictable ways. The fae do not dwell there. Nothing sane dwells there . . . only monsters."

Her smile wavers. "So, definitely no picnics."

I turn away, striding swiftly through the night. A stand of trees ahead, tall, skeletal pines, appear like spears against the starry sky. Magic emanates from them in subtle waves, almost too faint to be detected but present. Ward witches always plant themselves near magic sources. We will find a path into Wanfriel among those trees.

The Miphata still trails at my heels. "Do you know how to get to this— What did you call it again? Wyndithas Gate?" she demands.

"I do."

"That's a mercy at least. Care to share?"

"No." I don't want to share. I don't want to talk. I don't want to interact with her any more than I can help. I don't want anything to strengthen the chains I already feel so inextricably binding me to this girl. I must avoid her as much as possible—which, granted, will be difficult if we're to survive a seven-day quest together.

Jaws clenched, I stride on and into the pine forest. The night is deep within the shadows of those trees. Though my natural fae sight augments my vision, I am a fae of the Dawn Court. I am not comfortable in darkness. I progress more carefully, my gaze darting as I search the pine-straw-littered ground between the trunks and roots.

"What are you doing?" The girl stumbles along behind me. "Are you looking for something?"

"Yes."

"You'd better tell me. I can't help if you stay all close-lipped like this."

She's right, of course. Not that I expect any help from a mortal. She's far less suited to this darkness than I am. Still, it doesn't pay to hold my tongue.

"I'm looking for a *nilya*," I say.

"A nilya? You mean . . . Hold on, I think I know that one. You mean a crocus? The flower?" She pauses a moment, and I hope she'll not pester me further. But then comes the inevitable, "Why?"

"It will show the way to the path we need."

71

I can hear her unspoken questions as she bites them back. I carefully move aside a pile of pine straw with one foot, searching beneath for the telltale bloom, sniffing the air for a trace of its scent.

"Well, I think I can help you, anyway."

I stop, turning back to look at the girl again. "Help me? How?"

She smiles. She can't really see me in the shadows, so her smile does not hit its mark directly. Nevertheless, the flashing brilliance is almost enough to knock me back a step. Before I've recovered my breath, she reaches up to pull something from behind her ear. Something that glows faintly at the touch of her slim fingers. Something she cups close to her mouth as she begins to whisper.

The glow intensifies.

The girl lowers her hands, stretches them out before her, then turns, swinging her arms and her cupped hands to the right. "This way," she says, and sets off at a quick, confident pace through the shadows and the trees.

At first, I'm too surprised to react. Then, realizing I will lose her among the pines if I don't hurry, I lurch into motion. What in the worlds is she doing? What does she think she knows? Is this some Miphates spell? It doesn't feel like written magic—indeed, it feels much more natural, not unlike fae magic.

"Ah! Here we are." The girl's voice is bright as a bell ahead. I part pine boughs and see her kneeling in a glow of pale blue light. Her eyes gleam as she looks up at me and points at her find: a cluster of small cup-shaped purple blossoms with yellow centers. "Crocuses," she says. "Is this what you're looking for?"

My mouth hangs open with surprise. "How did you do that?" I could have searched the whole night through and into the next morning without finding the nilya blossoms.

She rises from her knees and approaches me, her hands cupped before her. "I asked," she says. "Look." She opens her hands.

A respenia bloom rests in her palms.

My eyes widen. My breath catches. I take an involuntary step back, raising one arm as though to shield myself. "Where did you get that?" The words burst from my lips in a bark. "How did you come by that flower?"

She frowns, her gaze questioning. "It's an heirloom. It's been in my family for generations—"

"Put it away!" I beg, shaking my head hard. "Get it out of sight. I beg you!"

"All right. I'm sorry, I . . . I didn't know . . ." Her words trail off as she lifts the blossom to her head. It tucks itself into her hair, pulling strands over its bright face until I can no longer see it. But I know it's there.

I tear my gaze from that spot behind her ear and meet her eyes. She's holding back her questions again . . . and reading far too much in my face. Can she guess what I'm feeling? Has the connection binding our souls given her access to my most private thoughts? I can only hope not.

Then again, it's not as though anything so very bad has happened. It's just a flower. That's all. It doesn't actually *mean* anything.

I draw myself upright and harden my jaw. "We will proceed," I say, my voice firm. "Walk behind me as the path opens, and do not stray."

With these words, I brush past her and approach the nilya blossoms. I begin to circle them clockwise, reaching out with my senses, and quickly locate the traces of magic surrounding this place. Although more abundant here than anywhere else in this small forest, the magic is so hidden behind layers of reality that I might easily have missed the signs. Reaching out now with my magically attuned senses, I grasp hold and walk on, circling the cluster of blooms.

I've completed two circles before I realize the Miphata is not following me. I pause and look around. She stands beyond the circle of magic I tread, watching me. One of her dark eyebrows slides up her forehead.

"Why are you not following me?" I demand.

"Um . . ." She juts her chin. "What are you doing?"

"What does it look like I'm doing? I'm opening a path."

She looks blank.

"A path," I repeat and gesture vaguely with one hand. "Through Wanfriel?"

She shakes her head.

How ignorant is this girl? Even ward witches know about such things. But then, she's not a witch; she's a Miphata. And the Miphates tend to devote themselves to those magics pertaining to their own small, human world. They don't bother with the details of Eledria and the workings of the worlds and the ways between worlds. Perhaps she has simply never heard of Wanfriel.

I heave a sigh, frustrated to feel the magic I've gathered slipping away. But I'll recover it soon enough. And I can't very well drag the girl into the space between realities without some warning.

"Wanfriel Forest connects all the worlds of Eledria . . . including this world. Its paths cross through the Hinter Realms, allowing swift travel between worlds and locations. My people long since learned to navigate its secret ways, to move rapidly just outside of time. Different paths lead to and from different gates—some people devote their entire lives to learning and chronicling these ways. The simplest path to Wyndithas is by nilya blossoms, such as these we have found. I must perform the spell to open, then we may walk the path to the gate in mere moments—though it may feel longer while we are on the path itself."

She listens silently, her eyes widening as she takes in the enormity of what I say. Some of her bravado melts away. "Will it . . . will it be safe for me to walk? Through the Hinter, I mean?"

So she knows that name at least. And it's enough to give her pause.

"You should be safe," I answer. Though in truth, I'm not altogether certain. Even among the fae it takes years, sometimes decades of practice to learn to walk these paths safely. They can be treacherous, deadly. "I will help you," I add and hold out my hand. "Walk with me."

She stares at my hand, momentarily uncertain. Then, slowly, she reaches out and places her fingers in mine.

And once again, I feel that spark, that painful jolt when our skin touches. It's stronger now even than it was when we clasped hands in the boat. Is the connection between us really strengthening so quickly? What will it be like by the end of seven days and seven nights?

Will I be able to do what I must?

Of course. I am not some weak-hearted swain, ready to swoon and die over a ladylove. I am King of Aurelis. I am hard, unmerciful. I am strength and mastery and might.

I shall conquer this.

Firming my grip on her hand, I turn away and begin to lead her. Around the nilyas we go, once, twice. I reach out with my senses, gathering magic to me, working the ancient spell that lingers in this place.

A third time around, and the blossoms at our feet seem to shift slightly. Suddenly, the shadow they cast grows, shooting out in a straight, dark line that seems to extend forever. The pine trees on either side slide away, making room as the path opens before us.

With a gasp, the girl tugs at my hand, pulling me to a stop. "Is it quite safe?" she asks, breathless.

I look down at her anxious face as she stares into that knife-sharp shadow cutting through realities, from this world and across so many others. How does it appear to her vision? Does she merely see the shadow extending through endless miles of pine trees? Or does she glimpse the wide, unknowable plains of the Hinter Realms at the edges of her vision?

She takes a step nearer to me. I fight the urge to put my arm around her, to draw her to my side.

"You will be safe so long as you walk with me," I answer. "Stay close now."

I begin to walk, leading her with me. We seem simply

to stroll between columns of tall, dark trees. The scent of pine surrounds us, and a faint wind stirs the branches. But sometimes that wind brings with it scents of other things—nameless vast spaces, impossibly far horizons. Beings and forms of existence beyond knowing. I don't have to warn her not to strain her gaze to try to see what cannot and should not be seen; she presses close to me now, her head actually resting on my shoulder. When I let myself glance down at her face, her eyes are closed. She is trusting me completely to guide her. Trusting me, in this moment, more than she trusts herself.

Something warm stirs in my heart. Something dangerous.

"You know," she says suddenly, breaking the silence between us, "there's one thing I don't understand."

She is trying to fill this stillness and divert her mind. Trying to fight off the threatening, encroaching madness of the Hinter. Smart girl.

"What don't you understand?" I ask, willing to be her distraction if that's what she needs.

"Why didn't you kill me? During our fight, I mean. You had me at your mercy . . . and Ilestriesa could do nothing about it."

She wants to talk about this? Now? She wants to reminisce about our first meeting and our attempt to destroy one another? Well, perhaps she needs something vicious enough to truly distract her from her current circumstances. Who am I to judge?

"It's the Fatebond," I answer grimly. "I cannot kill my bond-mate. If I were to cause your death—either by action or inaction—I would in turn kill myself."

She sniffs. "I figured it was something like that. At the time, I couldn't understand it at all. You aren't exactly known for your mercy across the worlds."

My lip curls. "Mercy is not a virtue in a king."

"No, perhaps not." She shakes her head against my shoulder, and I hear her draw a shuddering breath. "But mercy is the virtue of a great man. In fact, I'm not sure a man can be truly strong, truly great if he cannot also be merciful and gentle."

Her words are like daggers digging into my heart. Who is she to talk so to me? I'm tempted to pull away from her, shake free of her hand. Let her face on her own the terrors of this path we walk and see who she thinks is great or strong then.

Instead, I find myself saying, "Your ideas are strange, Miphata. Surely never a man who breathed has met your description of greatness."

"My father did."

"What?"

She sighs, a sound soft and sweet enough to break the heart. I nearly stagger and must take care not to break my pace as I follow the shadow path. Her voice continues, musing and distant as though she no longer speaks to me.

"My father was a great man. A gentle man. He was strong enough not to fear humility. Strong enough not to fear the kindness in his nature. All who knew him respected him. Honored him. Served him with love." She goes silent for a time. I almost wonder if she's finished. I hope she is.

But she adds at the last, "He was by far the strongest man I've ever known."

My heart twists with the unexpected pain. I want to press a hand to my breast, half convinced it will come away wet with blood. Gods on high, why should such foolish words hurt so badly?

Why do I find myself wishing—suddenly, painfully, terribly wishing—that she would say such things about me?

The path ends abruptly. Visually it seems to stretch on forever through that endless pine forest. But I feel its end, feel the thin place where we may step through into Eledria.

I feel the Gate of Wyndithas just on the other side.

Dread of the ward witch's ill-spoken words crashes down on me. Somehow she knew. She knew that of all places to begin this journey, Wyndithas would be the most terrible for me. Did Kyriakos tell her? Did she use her witchly magic to detect my weakness? Or is it simply an unfortunate coincidence, a trick of the gods as they attempt to keep me in their intended Fatebond?

"What's wrong?" the girl asks.

I can't tell her. After all this talk of strength and weakness, I can't let her know how deeply I dread what lies before me. My only hope is to steel myself, bolster my courage, and push on through so quickly that my fear has no opportunity to overcome me. So that's what I will do.

"Nothing," I say. Then, "We're here."

"Oh?" She lifts her head from my shoulder and slowly opens her eyes. "I . . . I think I feel something. Is this the end of the path?"

Her intuition is good. In time, she could become a talented path-walker.

"Yes. Get ready now."

I give her a moment to brace. Then, with a quick, unhesitating stride, I step through, pulling her behind me. We emerge from the path into crystalline air and brilliant, cloudless blue sky. Wind smacks our faces, freezing cold, and stinging with droplets of ice water. I blink hard and strain to keep my gaze from dropping. But the harder I try, the more my eyes seem weighted down, drawn against their will.

I look. Down toward my feet.

My heart catches in my throat.

We stand on the brink of Wyndithas Falls—a crashing waterfall of ice and rushing water that spills over the cliff's edge at our feet into an endless chasm of foam. The unimaginable distance, the endless space—the fall, the inexorable fall—yawns before me.

My gaze darkens. Sickness floods my limbs. I pitch, pivot, sink to my knees. I cannot breathe. I cannot think. I can scarcely bear to exist so near the edge of such a plunge.

Kyriakos alone knows my fear of heights. He learned it long ago when we were children. Did he tell the ward witch? Did he betray me?

"What's wrong?"

I realize the Miphata has been speaking for some time. Her voice is all but inaudible above the roar of those falls. She is crouched beside me, one arm around my shoulders, her soft lips pressed close to my ear.

"Lodírhal!" she screams, trying to be heard. "Lodírhal, what's wrong?"

I turn to her. She's so close our noses touch, and our lips are scarcely inches apart. I stare into her eyes, struggling to make myself focus, to make myself see her.

"The . . . the gate!" I shout. She turns her head, putting her ear close to my mouth. "The gate! It's here . . . just beyond the brink."

She frowns, turns, and peers out over the edge of the falls. I try to look as well, to gain a sense of the magic circle shining in midair that will lead us from this place into the Goran Desolation. But I can't. I can't make sense of anything. Even my magic perceptions have succumbed to the tumult of terror pulsing in my veins.

But the girl leans close to my ear again. "I see it. I think I can get us through. Can you stand?"

I shake my head. I can't stand. I can't do anything.

I'm weak. I'm so weak.

"Come on," she shouts. "Chin up! It's only a single step. We'll be through before you know. Get to your feet, you great lunk."

I'm quivering so hard, I expect my bones to separate. But somehow, when she tugs and pulls on my shoulders, when she wraps an arm around my stomach and heaves, my limbs obey. I gather my legs, rise, find my balance, lean heavily against her. A moan escapes my lips.

She shall weaken every strength.

It's her. It's her fault.

She will be the death of me.

I'll take the step. And I'll fall. Fall forever. Never cease to fall . . .

Her hand touches my cheek. A shock shoots straight to the quick of my soul, sharp enough to startle me into awareness. I turn at the pressure of her palm and look down into her eyes.

"That's right."

I can't hear her, but I feel her voice ripple along the thread of connection between our souls.

"That's right. Look at me. Only at me. Come on. Come on now."

I take a step. Guided by her hand. Led by her gaze.

There's so much strength in her. Strength I hadn't realized she possessed.

I'd seen and been dazzled by the might of Ilestriesa. But the Warrior has nothing on this girl.

"Come on!" she urges. "One more step. Just one more."

I feel the yawning draw of the drop. I feel the pressure of power from the tumbling, churning waters. Yet I hold her gaze. And she holds mine.

She shall strengthen every weakness.

Is this what the soothsayer meant? I always assume the words of the prophecy foretold how she would break me, how she would destroy me. I never thought . . . I never dreamed . . .

Panic thrills through my gut. I realize we are on the very edge with no more space between us and the fall.

"Look at me." She catches my face between her hands, forces me to stare into her eyes. They are gray-blue and so clear, like fresh mountain dew on river stones. "Come on . . . come . . ."

Together, we take the step.

For one terrifying instant, I feel the unending vast-ness below me. For one terrifying instant, I believe the fall has already claimed me and feel the sickness of that plummet overwhelm me.

Then we are falling together through a brilliant burst of light straight from the *quinsatra*. I wrap my arms around her, clinging to her in my fear. But when she embraces me in return, I feel such a surge of courage, of confidence issuing straight from her soul into mine. I glory in the feeling.

But then we hit the ground hard, tumble apart, and roll across a rough, stony landscape. I lose my hold on her and continue rolling until I slow to a stop, lying on my back. Staring up into a spinning, magic-torn sky.

We're here. We've made it.

The Goran Desolation.

"Miphata?" The word bursts from my lips in a rough bark. I lift my head, groan, close my eyes, then try again. "Miphata, are you all right?"

"Over here."

I turn at the sound of her voice. She lies face down several steps away, her skirts askew around her bare calves. She waves one hand, lifts her head, and meets my gaze. "I'm all right. I'm in one piece." Arms trembling, her hair falling in a dark cascade over one shoulder, she pushes up onto her hands and knees. A little huff of a laugh bursts from her lips. "I won't lie, that was probably the most—"

Her voice is cut off by a piercing, wild, utterly unnat-ural shriek.

DASYRA

*S*pines burst from the hard soil, emerging one after another in a series of eruptions. With a shake of shoulders, a head pulls free, trailing long coils of matted black hair and set with far too many eyes. Five, eight, ten . . . and all but one of them swollen, red, putrid, and unseeing.

Only the centermost eye sparks with life. And its gaze is fixed on Lodírhal.

The thing—whatever it is—shrieks again, the sound tearing from a tortured throat that gapes with huge open wounds, revealing the tendons and bones inside. With a roll of one shoulder it yanks an arm free, scattering rocks and dirt in a cloud. Three-foot-long claws curl from the ends of skeletal fingers outlined momentarily in sharp silhouette against the brilliance of the magic-tortured sky.

Those fingers swipe down at Lodírhal, intending to pin him through the chest into the dirt.

At the last possible moment, the fae king rolls. My

heart stops and begins to beat again as I watch him leap to his feet, graceful as a cat, his hands poised before him. His head angles upward, his golden eyes fixed on the being above him. Gone is the trembling, pale shadow of a man I'd witnessed mere moments ago on the edge of the Wyndithas Falls. He's once more that terrible being I faced on the battlefield, the ferocious fighter, a tiger without mercy. His hand goes for the knife at his belt, sweeping back the folds of his long cloak.

The flash of fabric draws the creature's gaze. As it turns its hideous head, all those pus-rimmed eyes blink, but the one bright eye focuses intently. Its free arm lashes out again, and Lodírhal springs to avoid it. Only this time, one long claw catches in his cloak, yanks him from the air, and smashes him into the dirt. The monster drags him closer even as it fights to free its other arm and body from the dirt. Lodírhal twists, struggles. I hear a loud rip, and the cloak falls into two pieces. The fae king rolls free.

By now I'm on my feet, staring open-mouthed. Useless. As if I don't belong in this moment, cannot belong in this moment. I might as well be disembodied, watching from somewhere far off.

But I can't do that. I can't *be* that. I must help.

My hand reaches impulsively for the amulet. But no! It's gone. Lodírhal has it tucked into the front of his doublet. Gods help me, what am I supposed to do?

The creature—the wild-magic being—reaches its free hand and, with surprising delicacy, picks Lodírhal up by one ankle. The fae king hangs suspended in the air as the being swings him toward its hideous face. He twists, struggles, trying to find some leverage to free himself. His knife slashes uselessly, his reach not quite long enough.

I move before I even know what I'm going to do, yanking the shoe from my foot. I take five running strides, scarcely noticing how the ruthless rocks tear into my unprotect sole. "Hey!" I shout. "Hey, over here! Hey, hey!"

The creature does not hear me. And then . . . oh, gods! Then its torso splits. Its ribcage opens like a long, vertical maw. I see broken rib bones like teeth that champ together, dripping blood and ooze and torn flesh. A blast of cruel stench bursts forth, powerful enough to knock me off my feet.

I scream. I can't help myself. The horror is too over-whelming.

But that scream does the trick. The blind, swollen eyes roll, and the one good eye flashes. The creature swings its long arm out to one side, dangling Lodírhal, so that it can fix its gaze on me.

Oh, great.

Now what?

No time for hesitation. With a roar, I take three more lunging strides, draw back my arm, and hurl my shoe with all the force I can muster. I aim for the head, but my throw isn't nearly strong enough. Instead, the shoe bounces off one of those toothlike rib bones and falls into the gaping torso-mouth.

The creature spasms. Chokes?

Then it flings Lodírhal to one side, his limbs flailing uselessly as he soars through the air. Something small slips from the front of his doublet and away, something that glints as it catches the *quinsatra* light. My amulet.

An indescribably horrendous sound jerks my attention back to that monstrous thing. Its body heaves, convulses . . . and then it spits out my shoe, soaked with green ooze that sizzles as it eats into the soft leather. I don't have long to stare, for the being utters another of those earsplitting shrieks and hauls its other arm up out of the earth, dragging its huge haunches behind it. It hunches over, its torso momentarily closed, its head hanging at a bizarre angle from its wounded neck, its eyes rolling as it turns slowly, this way and that.

The good eye fixes on me.

I run. I stagger to the right, wincing in pain from my bare foot at every step. I want so desperately to turn and try to put as much distance between this creature and myself as I possibly can.

Instead, I aim for Lodírhal's stunned body lying some yards away . . . and that glint on the ground between us. All my hope focuses on that small, shining object. Can I move fast enough? Can I get there in time?

The monster surges into motion, lurching straight toward me. I stop and pull back, narrowly avoid a massive, swinging arm. Claws tear into the hard soil, sending cracks shooting in every direction. I stagger, stumble, and only just manage to keep my feet. The wild-magic being turns its awful head. The pus-rimmed eyes roll, the good eye searches. It tugs at its own arm, trying to get free, but for the moment its claws are stuck too deep.

"Miphata!"

The clear, golden voice rings out, cutting through the stench, the terror, the overwhelming hugeness of that creature. I tear my gaze away and see Lodírhal standing tall. He draws his arm back and throws something that arcs over the head of the monster and falls, trailing a delicate chain.

I raise both hands and catch my amulet. For an instant I feel a thrill of pure joy.

Then the creature yanks its claws free. Its body moves in unnatural contortions, turning toward me. A scream rips from my throat. I run. My limping feet pound the hard soil while my fingers search along the sigils carved into the amulet face. I feel the magic swelling in them and more magic surging all around me, in the atmosphere of this world that lies much too close to the *quinsatra* realm. More magic than I've ever known, than I've ever imagined, waits here to be summoned. If I say the spell incorrectly, I'll drown myself in an uncontrollable river of pure *quinsatra* force.

I can't do it. I can't work the spell. Fear chokes me, blocks my power.

The ground beneath me vibrates as the wild-magic creature's limbs thud behind me. I know I shouldn't turn, shouldn't give in to the temptation. I must focus forward and run, run, run.

But I can't stop myself. I look back.

That split-torso mouth gapes over me, closing in fast, blocking out even the vibrant light of the *quinsatra*-torn sky. I gag as another blast of foul stench belching from the core of its being knocks me to my knees. Screaming, I throw my arms up over my head.

A flash of gold.

My eyes, almost blinded by fear, lift just enough to see

Lodírhal land on the creature's shoulders. His legs wrap around its neck, and his knife flashes in the magic light an instant before plunging straight into that one good eye. Blood and pus gush forth. The creature shrieks. Its great clawed hands rise to tear Lodírhal from its shoulders, but he ducks and hurls himself backward, hanging by one of the spines down its back.

His voice reaches me as though from another world: "Call up the Warrior! Call up the Warrior!"

Something inside me tightens. Strength hardens into a tight knot in my breast. I spring back several paces, plant my feet, close my eyes, run my fingers along the spell sigils. Concentration should be impossible, yet in that moment I am nothing but the words echoing inside my head.

"*Tanatar, wynal-ha.*"

The *quinsatra* swells disastrously around me. The spirit within the amulet stirs in response.

"*Anaerin, mir yinthana.*"

I feel it, the magic flowing through me. The Warrior rising, rising. Overwhelming, all-consuming. Beautiful and terrible and unstoppable.

Her name bursts from my lips like a bolt of lightning: "*ILESTRIESA!*"

A crack like thunder splits the world.

With my head thrown back, I stare through the thin veils of reality into that rent in the worlds, a rent far greater than I've ever seen before, opening wide to the forces of the magic dimension. My eyes widen just before a torrent of pure magic descends upon me. For an instant, I'm certain I'll be utterly obliterated.

Then Ilestriesa rises. Her axes swing overhead, crossing in a flash of light. The magic stream strikes the blades, splits, and spills onto either side as I feel again that strange and wondrous sensation I've long sought to master, to understand—that two-fold strain of existence. I am reduced, I am small, I am almost nothing as another, greater spirit overtakes my very essence. My body is here, my soul is here—but all is subsumed in the greatness of the Warrior.

Ilestriesa opens her mouth and utters a ululating battle cry.

Struggling to focus my gaze through the storm-like spirit substance surrounding me, I can just discern the monster turning this way, its bloodied eyes sightless but its awareness of danger evident in every line of its grotesque body. It raises its claws, whether in defiance or defense, I cannot say.

The Warrior surges into motion, hurtling across the desolate plain, her axes swinging. It's like being carried along by a wild horse—I can only hold on. But hold on I must. This is my great task as the Vessel. If I let go, if I fail to provide the habitation Ilestriesa requires, the Warrior cannot manifest in all her glory. I must hold on even as the raw magic channeling from the *quinsatra* batters my body and soul until I fear I will drown in the sheer force of it.

Ilestriesa's right arm lashes out. The monster blocks, catching the ax in its huge claws. But the second ax is already swinging in an upward stroke. It cuts straight through the monster's gaping torso, breaks through bone, and emerges from its shoulder. A hideous cry shreds the air, loud enough that I hear it even through the throb of magic pulsing through my senses.

Suddenly, my vision sharpens, cuts through the shimmering aura of the Warrior's essence. I see something like living energy in a form I cannot at first discern. Then it resolves itself into a familiar shape. Lodírhal! Still clinging to that spiny back. He stares at the Warrior over the creature's bloodied shoulder, his face pale and spattered with blood.

Ilestriesa shakes her ax free of the monster's claws and draws it back.

"No!" I cry and throw myself, body and soul, into opposition, desperately trying to halt the Warrior's stroke. But I'm no match for this level of magic.

The ax swings.

Straight for the monster's neck.

Straight for Lodírhal's head.

I'm helpless to stop it.

At the last possible instant, Lodírhal pushes off from the creature's shoulder, performing an elegant backflip through the air. The flash of the silver ax narrowly misses him as it hews through flesh, muscle, and bone, cutting off the monster's last scream.

For a moment, the wild-magic being stands frozen in place. Its sightless eyes stare blankly, unbelieving. Then its head rolls and *thunks* to the ground. The body falls in a heap of broken ruin.

I stare down at it. At the death I've caused. My heart beats dully—once, twice. Thrice.

Then searing magic light floods my head, floods every sense, burning me inside and out. I try to scream.

Collapsing to my knees, I drag the Warrior down with me. This magic—it's too great. It's too much. I cannot survive.

I will break into a thousand pieces and scatter across the worlds. And Ilestriesa can do nothing to protect me.

LODÍRHAL

I shake blood-matted hair out of my eyes just in time to see the wild-magic being collapse under the Warrior's blow. Her ax blade hangs poised, its arc of destruction complete, and for a moment I am captured by that image of pure, unadulterated strength.

Then Ilestriesa collapses.

Her whole glowing, glorious image shudders and falls, losing definition to become nothing more than a whorl of spirit-essence and magic. At first, it's too bright, too chaotic, for me to see anything else. But when I strain my vision, I can just discern the young Miphata on her knees within that storm. Her head is thrown back. Her arms flung out wide. Her mouth is open, and her throat seems to strain in a scream that I cannot hear. Magic blazes in two hot beams straight from her eyes.

It's this place. The Goran Desolation is too close to the *quinsatra* for spells like the summoning she just performed to be safe. Gods blight me, I should have known! I should never have urged her to call upon the Warrior.

And if she dies . . .

I leap to my feet and rush toward her, springing over the monster's fallen body. The storm of magic surrounding her is not unlike the churning magic in the sky overhead. She seems to be caught in a maelstrom rising from her soul. But she's still there, alive, down in the center.

I pause a few steps away, my hands up to shield my face against the glare. If I stay here long, the magic will seep into me, killing me if I'm lucky. If I'm unlucky, it will simply morph me into a being like the one Ilestriesa just slew. I should run now, put as much distance as I can between myself and this girl.

But I can't let her die. Not when there's still something I might do about it.

My gaze moves from her glowing face to the amulet floating in the moving air before her face.

I grit my teeth. There's a chance . . . a slim chance . . .

I plunge into the whorl of magic. Its blast blinds me, shocking me to the core. I'll lose all reason in another moment. But I force my feet to take another step, reaching out with one hand, wildly, blindly.

My fingers wind around a chain.

A cry bursting from my throat, I wrench hard. The chain breaks. The amulet comes free in my hand. There's a great clap of light and—

I blink. The sky is above me, distant and full of movement. As my vision slowly clears, the blackness of momentary unconsciousness retreating, I see the rent in the worlds knitting back together. The veil is still too thin, terribly thin, and the magic of the *quinsatra* is far too close for comfort. But for the moment . . . I breathe out a long sigh. For the moment at least, we are out of danger.

With a painful heave, I roll onto my side. My fist still clutches the amulet on its chain. The circular charm still glows bright from the force of magic that just passed through its sigils. But the glow is fading, so I stuff it into the front of my doublet, marveling that my hand is free of burns. Only then do I search for the girl.

She lies on her side not ten feet from me, her face turned so that I cannot see it. She looks limp. Broken.

An inarticulate cry croaks from my throat. I rise, stumble, fall, and right myself again. Staggering to her side, I sink heavily to my knees. My hand trembles more than I like to admit as I take hold of her shoulder and roll her toward me.

She's breathing. She's alive.

Air I hadn't realized I was holding escapes my lungs in a rush. I bow my head, close my eyes . . . and feel suddenly, painfully, that tightness around my heart where an unwanted but undeniable cord of connection binds me. Shuddering, I place a hand on my breast, trying to force that pain away. But I can't. I came so close to losing her . . .

"No!" The word snarls between my clenched teeth. I sit upright and close my eyes, my hands curling into fists. I cannot let myself think this way, *feel* this way. It's not real. It's only the Fatebond. It has nothing to do with my true desires, my true self.

And yet . . . and yet . . .

Slowly, almost unwillingly, I open my eyes and let my gaze seek out her face. Smeared with dirt and blood. A magic burn across one cheek. Her brow puckers with pain even in her unconscious state.

I reach out one finger and softly brush a tendril of hair from her forehead.

To LINGER in this place would be suicide.

Since I cannot wait for the Miphata to wake, I scoop her up in my arms and cradle her head against my shoulder. Turning my back on the carcass of the wild-magic being, I set out, my face aimed toward the far horizon. This world has no sun, nothing to reveal direction. Roiling magic in the atmosphere provides the only light.

But I trust my keen senses to guide me. There's a gate not far off, merely a few miles. A gate out of this realm, out of this gods-forsaken horror. If I'm quick—and if the gods are with me—perhaps we'll get out of here alive.

Overhead, the *quinsatra* churns. Rising pressure indicates an impending storm. If the Miphata and I are not gone by then, we will be caught in an onslaught of magic we cannot survive.

I forge on, carrying the unconscious girl across the grim landscape. Several times I spy more wild-magic creatures lumbering in the distance, beings as strange or stranger than the one we faced. My first impulse is to summon a glamour to shield us. But that would be disastrous. Any use of magic will quickly erupt beyond my control, drawing those creatures straight to us.

So, I duck low to the ground, holding the Miphata close, shielding her with my body. I watch the beings, willing them not to turn, not to look our way. Perhaps the gods are with us after all, for the monsters do not stop. Soon I rise, readjust my grip on my slight burden, and continue doggedly onward.

The atmosphere grows heavier by the moment, becoming difficult to breathe. Now and then I feel an uncomfortable blast of magic against the backs of my neck and my knees. Once I stumble and nearly drop the girl. Instead, I land hard on one knee, unconsciously pressing her close to my heart. My head bows over hers, and I breathe in her scent—the delicate perfume of respenia blossoms that permeates her hair. It's enough to drive out the overwhelming magic. To fill my senses with sweetness.

It's . . . intoxicating.

Gods above, what have I become?

With a growl, I regain my feet and hasten onward. I won't be undone. Not by a trick of fate. Not by the whims of all the gods in all the heavens. I am not such a fool.

Ahead, a river cuts across the landscape. At first I take no notice of it, but then my interest quickens. Is that a gate I sense? Yes! Yes, there, I feel it pulsing in the air above the far bank. A gate out of this wretched plain of existence, a gate back into Wanfriel. We might just make it. We might just . . .

My heart falters. The river is wide, a mile across at the least. And it's not just any river. This water is so infused with raw magic that it's noxious, deadly. Even a stray splash on exposed skin could prove disfiguring. To attempt swimming it would be disastrous.

Perhaps I should walk either upriver or downstream in search of a way across. But . . . no. No, my instincts have not led me astray. There's a bridge suspended across that rapid flow. Narrow, made of rope and rough-hewn planks, many of which are broken. I can't possibly carry the Miphata across on that.

Letting out a heavy sigh, I sink to my knees again and gently lay my burden on the ground. She breathes evenly, and her knotted brow has smoothed. In fact, she looks peaceful. As though being carried in my arms restored and comforted her body and soul.

I shake that idea out of my head and bend toward her. "Miphata?"

She doesn't respond. I lean closer and gently touch her cheek. Her skin is soft and smooth beneath the layers of dirt and blood. I run my thumb along her jawline. "Miphata, can you hear me?"

Her brow puckers. She groans and turns toward my hand, as though nuzzling into it. My breath catches.

Then, growling in my throat, I yank my hand away. I can't fall for this. I *won't* fall for this. I refuse to be weak. I know what's going on here, and I know what I must accomplish. Nothing can sway me from my purpose. Nothing.

"Miphata. Wake." This time I give her shoulder a rough shake. Her dark lashes flutter, and with a flash of clear blue grey, her eyes stare up at me. I find my breath stolen away once more.

"Wh-what happened?" Her lips are cracked, dry. The

full lower lip bleeds from a cut in the center. She licks it, grimaces at the taste of blood, and pushes up onto her elbow. "I . . . Where is . . ." Her eyes widen, and one hand fumbles to her breast, her throat, searching frantically.

"Here." I remove the amulet from the front of my doublet and let it spin on its chain before her gaze. "I took it again."

To my surprise, her face melts into an expression of utmost relief. "Thank you," she whispers. Then, still more surprising, her brow wrinkles and her bleeding lip trembles. She makes a valiant effort to stop it, even clamping a hand over her mouth. Tears begin to pour down her cheeks. She sits up, dashing them away viciously, but more fall, trickling through the dirt and grime.

What is this? Why is she weeping? I stare at her, aghast, though I can't quite say why. What am I supposed to do? I don't recall the last time I saw a fae woman weep openly. It's simply not done. I should be revolted. Yet I cannot deny the powerful urge to reach out and draw her into my arms. To press her head against my shoulder and offer her the comfort she seemed to enjoy while unconscious. My hands begin to move.

The Miphata sniffs loudly, wiping the back of her hand across her face, then looks at me, her eyes flashing through the sheen of tears. "It's dead, isn't it," she says.

It takes me a moment to guess what she's talking about. "Oh," I say. "The wild-magic being? Yes. Ilestriesa killed it."

She nods, tries to speak, chokes on her own words, and quickly turns away from me to scan the landscape.

When she sees the river, I watch her gaze lift beyond the water to the shore on the far side. She's sensed the gate.

"Is that where we cross?" she asks. "Back into Wanfriel, I mean?"

"Yes."

Though I wouldn't have expected it, she scrambles to her feet. I offer a hand in support, but she steps away so quickly to avoid my touch that she almost falls. Righting herself, she draws her shoulders back and lifts her chin. Her gaze rises to the churning sky.

"Looks like a storm's about to break," she says, her voice still quavering slightly. "We'd best get out of here while we still can."

"My thoughts exactly." I sweep an arm, indicating the rickety bridge, which looks ready to fall to pieces at the slightest breath. "Ladies first?"

She raises an eyebrow. Then, without a word, she marches down to the river's edge, her back straight, her stride limping but confident. I watch her go. Watch the sway of her hips, the swing of her arms, the firm set of her shoulders.

And I realize that I've stopped breathing yet again.

DASYRA

I don't think I'll ever get used to the sensation of passing through these gates between worlds. It feels like a very thin, very precise knife slicing away only the topmost layer of my skin. It doesn't *hurt*, exactly . . . but a cold shiver that's *akin* to pain covers me from head to toe as I plunge through the thin place in reality and fall back into the strange Wanfriel Forest.

I take two steps, cry out, and fall to my knees, where I stay drawing deep breaths as the throb in my bare foot slowly abates. Deep, deep breaths of air that is blessedly clear of ravaging wild magic. When I open my eyes, it's not to the glare of a brewing magic storm but to the softness of green shadows beneath sheltering trees.

Grimacing, I reach down to touch my sore foot. My hand comes away sticky with blood. Ugh! I must have stepped on a sharp rock somewhere along the way. Before Lodírhal scooped me up and carried me across the Desolation in his arms.

My face heats. Memory of those strong arms enfolds

me. I was unconscious for most of it, but here and there I floated into *almost* awareness, just enough to know that I was being held. Just enough to take comfort in that strength, to listen to the pulse of his heartbeat . . .

I place a hand against my burning cheek, then give my head a quick shake. I definitely should not indulge in such thoughts.

Where is that gods-blighted fae anyway?

When I look back over my shoulder, I can't see the gate. From this side, it's completely invisible. And there's no sign of Lodírhal. He was only a few steps behind me on that treacherous bridge, but what does that even mean? Time passes strangely in the between of the worlds. For all I know, he won't arrive in this spot for another year. Hardly a pleasant thought. While I don't exactly relish my captor's company, the idea of being left alone in this otherworldly forest, lost between worlds, with no idea where I am or where I'm going . . . no. Just no.

Clumsily I stand and turn, favoring my wounded foot. I'm fairly certain I'm facing the gate now, though it's hard to know. I can't perceive it. Too bad I didn't think to bring any written spells with me on this little escapade. A spell to augment magic vision would certainly come in handy right about now.

Instead, I close my eyes. Last night, or whenever that was—it's difficult to keep track of time while traveling between worlds—in the boat, Lodírhal asked me if I knew his true name. When I searched for it, I felt a connection between us. Something sharp and strange.

Something undeniable. Would such a connection stretch through layers of realities?

Breathing slowly, focusing my awareness, I reach inside myself. Down into the depths of my soul, to the core where my heart beats. There it is, wrapped around my heart. Faint but present. A delicate thread that feels as though the least strain might snap it. Not exactly the stuff from which epic love stories are woven.

But when I stretch my awareness along that thread, I feel . . . I feel . . . an answering heartbeat. Not in this world.

Can you hear me?

I send my voice vibrating along the thread, experimenting with possibilities. At first, I think it failed. Then I feel a quickening. An interest.

It's me, I say, trying not to let my eagerness snap the thread. *It's Mage Rolim, your . . .* I hesitate to use the term. *Your Fatebonded.*

When the thread vibrates with a distinct pulse of irritation. I smile a little. The poor fae king is *not* keen on this whole Fatebinding situation. I'd be insulted if it weren't so funny.

Walk this way, I urge. His flash of irritation makes him easier to detect, and I'm able to send a stronger message. *Come on now. I don't want you to end up in the wrong part of—*

"Oof!"

I break off with a gasp as something emerges from midair, wraps strong arms around me, and tumbles me to the ground. The breath bursts from my lungs, and the world spins and goes momentarily dark.

When the spinning stops and my vision clears, I find myself lying in a tumble of limbs on the forest floor, staring up into a pair of intensely golden eyes mere inches from my own. Lodírhal. His long hair falls to frame his face and mine as well, shielding us in a shimmering veil. He's heavy on top of me. But he doesn't move. His breath is warm on my face. His eyes move slightly back and forth beneath his faintly puckered brow.

Then they drift down to focus on my lips.

Heat flares through my cheeks, radiates through my body. I feel alive in that moment, more alive even than when the whole raw force of the *quinsatra* flooded my soul. I feel powerful and weak simultaneously. As though I could break a stone heart in two with my bare hands . . . but in so doing, break myself as well.

Slowly, almost guiltily, I let my gaze slide down to his lips. Full and soft. Sensual. And so near to mine—

Gods-blighted fae glamour.

I set my jaw and plant a hand against his chest. "You're squashing me," I growl, though it's not true. He has carefully shifted his weight off me to rest on one elbow, even as his other hand grips my upper arm. I push him anyway, growling in my throat. He briefly resists, then rolls to one side and collapses onto his back, heaving a huge sigh.

I watch him lie still, staring up at the leaf-laced sky. After a few more breaths, he gathers himself and gracefully rises to his feet. Without looking at me, he studies the forest into which we've tumbled. "Our first day is at its end, Miphata," he says, tossing the words at me care-lessly. "Only six more remain."

Still on my back, I stare up through the branches. He's right. The bits of sky visible through the canopy of leaves are purpling with dusk. So strange! It certainly doesn't feel as if a whole day has passed. But then, how is anyone supposed to keep track of days and hours while slipping in and out of worlds?

"Well, good." I sit up, wince, and press a hand to the small of my back. I landed on a root when we fell over. It'll probably leave a bruise. "I don't know about you, but I could use a bite to eat. And a nap. And don't"—I glare up at him just as he turns his cold gaze my way—"*don't* say I've already had a nap. Being blasted into unconsciousness by a burst of raw magic after nearly being torn apart by a monster does *not* count."

He doesn't answer. I scramble awkwardly to my feet, dust off my skirts, and take a few steps toward him, wincing again.

A frown darkens his brow. "You're hurt."

"I'm fine," I mutter. "What about that nap?"

"We're not safe here. Not safe enough to sleep."

"Where *will* be safe?"

He narrows his eyes, studying me closely. I meet his gaze, refuse to look away . . . and refuse to let my eyes slide back down to the slight crook of his lips again either. I'm not some weak-kneed damsel he can charm.

He sweeps his arm in a grand gesture. "This way, Miphata, if you please."

I'll give him this much credit: He does slow his stride to accommodate my limping gait. Several times I even see his hand stretch out as though on impulse to take my arm, to offer support. I pretend not to notice. But I do. Each and every time.

Is it possible that this stern fae king who, so short a time ago, was hell-bent on ending my life, could be *worried* about me?

No. It's impossible. Only a fool would think that way.

We progress silently aside from my own staggering footfalls and labored breathing. The forest swiftly sinks into darkness, and my eyes struggle to adjust. Several times I half glimpse shadowy figures among the trees, but none approach. Perhaps they take one look at Lodírhal and think better of it. I certainly would.

"Here." My companion stops abruptly and gestures with one hand, indicating a large oak tree. It's so huge, the span of its branches creates an area of deep shade in which smaller trees and shrubs cannot flourish. "You may rest here for the night."

"Really?" I glance around uncertainly, having hoped for a proper shelter of some sort, a hovel or cave. Maybe a hospitable faerie creature willing to offer a reasonable bargain. "You're sure this will be safe? It's very . . . exposed."

Lodírhal nods. "Oaks are always safe for humans. And I will keep watch."

Arguing would be pointless, so I hobble to the massive bole and take a seat between two large roots. It's hardly the most comfortable I've ever been, but I'm so tired, I don't bother complaining. I nestle in, grimacing as pain shoots up my foot.

My stomach growls. Suddenly. Cavernously. I clap my hand against it.

"You're hungry?" Lodírhal still stands at the edge of the oak clearing. I can just discern his gleaming eyes in the last of the fading twilight.

I bite my lip, trying to hide a grimace. "I . . . don't suppose you happened to think of provisions for this little journey of ours?"

Lodírhal, after a moment of contemplative silence, turns suddenly, sniffing the air like a bloodhound. It's a bit annoying, to be honest. Just as I open my mouth to snap at him, he says, "Stay here."

The next moment, he's gone. Vanished into the shadows.

"Um." I bite back the urge to call for him. After all, sheltering oaks notwithstanding, it can't be smart to make loud noises in a place like Wanfriel. Those shadowy figures I glimpsed through the trees might not hesitate to pay me a visit now that Lodírhal isn't around to scare them off.

Shuddering, I tuck back against the trunk and wish he hadn't gone. Not just because of the monsters and the loneliness. While he was present, I could ignore the thoughts scratching at the back of my mind. Now that he's not here to distract me, they demand to be heard.

I killed today.

My heart gives a sickening lurch.

I killed for the first time.

Trying to convince myself that it was Ilestriesa and not me who did the actual killing makes no difference. *I* summoned the Warrior, knowing full well what would happen to that poor, horrible creature. Arguing that the death of such a suffering being was more merciful than cruel is equally useless. Mercy never once occurred to me. Only survival.

My hand creeps up to touch my breast and that place where I'm so used to feeling the Warrior's amulet. But it's missing. Oh, right: Lodírhal took it off me again. It's safely tucked into the front of his doublet. Should I request its return? After all, without it, we certainly wouldn't have survived the first of our seven adventures.

But . . . no. If he wants to hold onto it, let him. I don't want to carry that burden if I don't have to.

I wrap my arms around myself within the folds of my cloak, my shoulders bowed. Tears burn, and when I blink, they spill onto my cheeks. A faint purring vibration tickles my ear. Sniffling, I wipe tears from the end of my nose, then put up my hand. Little tendrils coil around my fingers. Gently, I lift the respenia blossom free of my hair and hold it near my face. It opens its delicate petals, shining clear blue light up at me. By that glow, I can see how browned the edges of its petals are.

I bite my lip and carefully lift the little blossom to my nose, inhaling its scent. It nestles against me for comfort. But I know that I'm not enough. I'm not what it needs.

Footsteps sound in the stillness. I lift my head and angle the blossom so that its light reveals Lodírhal entering the oak clearing. He stops short, his eyes widening as they focus on the respenia. Am I mistaken, or does the sight of the little bloom cause him . . . fear?

Fearful or otherwise, he recovers quickly, takes a few quick strides, and drops a little pouch on the ground beside me. "There," he says. "Eat. That will satisfy you for now."

Using my free hand, I poke the pouch open. It contains plump red berries of a kind I don't recognize. They're large and fat, and the scent is delicious. "You're certain they're safe?" I ask, glancing at Lodírhal as he settles on an upraised root near the clearing's edge. "For human consumption, I mean."

He grunts and nods without looking at me. Well, he did say that he cannot kill me by either action or inaction. So he must be fairly confident.

I pop a berry into my mouth and close my eyes as delightful sweetness floods my tongue. It's gorgeous! Not in the least bitter or tart. Purely sweet and wholesome, like a mouthful of summer. I eat a few more in quick succession, surprised to find my appetite quickly sated.

While I eat, the respenia blossom climbs around the fingers of my right hand. I tilt and turn it gently, taking care never to let it slip. I used to play this sort of game with it and its mate whenever I had free time.

"Your blossom." Lodírhal's abrupt voice draws my attention his way. "It does not look well."

I gaze sadly down at the little bloom. It sags, and I cup it in my palm, then tuck it safely into my hair behind my ear. It settles into its accustomed place, purring softly before going still. Its light flickers out, leaving me in near darkness. Only a faint trace of starlight makes its way through the branches overhead.

Lodírhal continues, relentless: "Respenia always come in pairs." As though I didn't know. "Where is the second blossom?"

I pull my lips in and bite down to repress the sob welling in my throat. Only when I'm certain my voice is under control do I answer softly, "Mage Jhaan . . . my master. He killed it. As punishment."

"Punishment for what?"

When I look up, I can see only the faint gleam of his eyes, but I hold his gaze. "For not killing you when I had the chance."

He doesn't speak for some while. We simply sit there in the darkness. Holding each other's gazes.

At last, he says, "One respenia cannot live long without its mate. Your act of mercy may have cost both their lives." I feel his question hum in the air between us before he speaks it, almost as though it vibrates along that thin thread connecting our hearts. "Was it worth it?"

I drop my gaze to my hands resting in my lap. Slowly my fingers tighten into fists. "I hope so." With a shake of my head, I lift my chin and meet his eyes once more. "I hope so, King Lodírhal of Aurelis."

He sits very still, there across from me. For a long moment he seems to be made of stone. Then he releases a strange, shuddering sigh. The sound contains no words, and yet . . . it communicates a surging depth of feeling. A feeling I cannot name. A feeling I cannot *dare* to name.

"Miphata," he says, "I—"

I rise abruptly. With a sweep of my cloak, I turn away from him to step over a bulging root, intending to circle to the far side of the tree. But I stumble, my bare foot landing hard on the painful cut. A cry bubbles up in my throat, and I fling out a hand for support against the tree trunk.

"You're in pain."

Lodírhal is suddenly in front of me. I feel the warmth of his nearness but keep my head down, refusing to look at him. I scowl, lifting my foot and rubbing it ruefully. "That's what I get for throwing away my own shoe. Hope that monster enjoyed its little snack."

The king's gaze is unnerving. How clearly can he see me? He's a fae of the Dawn Court, not of the Night, but I know he sees better in this gloom than I do.

"I might be able to help." His voice is like velvet, warm and golden in the darkness. "Ease the pain. Encourage healing. Will you permit me?"

I should refuse. Sharply. Strongly. I don't want him to think I need anything from him.

Then again, won't a refusal make me look even weaker? He might start thinking I'm afraid of him and his glamours. I can't have that. Not if I intend to survive this journey.

"Fine." I plop down on one of the lumpy roots, pull up my skirts by a few inches, and stick out my throbbing foot. "Do what you can, King Lodírhal. Though I don't see how glamour can be of much use in this instance."

He kneels before me. My eyes must be slowly adjusting to the descending night, for I can just discern the shape of him, his broad shoulders, his bowed head. He takes hold of my bare foot . . . and I shiver at his touch. Surprise, of course. And I'm chilly now, after sunset. That's all.

His fingers run along the inside curve of my foot, slowly, pressing into the flesh. He reaches my ankle and slips his hand up and around it, then slides his palm across the top down to my toes. Wherever his skin touches mine, warmth spreads. Warmth and a pleasant, tingling sensation that . . .

I gasp. I can almost, *almost* see little pinpricks of light dancing across my foot. Except, *see* isn't the right word. It's a sensation beyond ordinary perceptions. But undeniable. And delicious. Soothing.

Lodírhal turns his hand and passes it under the sole of my foot. I wince, thinking of the accumulated dirt, grime, and blood. But he doesn't hesitate. His hand is large, strong, and confident. The same prickling warmth now flows along my arch and sole, sparking particularly around the long cut that has caused me such pain. I close my eyes, my breath catching. Then I sigh deeply as the pain fades, fades, and finally disappears.

Slowly, I open my eyes again to see the top of Lodírhal's head. He is intent on his work. Not looking at me. Not seeing how my hand slowly rises from my lap and stretches out. How my fingers tremble with the desire to run through the long strands of his hair, pale and silver in the filtered starlight.

I stop.

In the same instant, he looks up.

Our eyes meet.

And I feel the thin thread wrapped around my heart tighten with sudden, painful force.

I can't move. I can't think. I don't even know what I want, what I hope for. We both sit frozen. Captured in an inexplicable instant.

Then, moving slowly, his fingers slide along my foot,

my ankle. Move to run lightly up my shin beneath my skirt. His fingertips brush my calf.

"Well now, that feels much better!" My voice rings out far too loud, breaking the stillness into a thousand tiny shards. I yank my foot out of his grasp and plant it firmly on the ground. No pain. The cut seems to have healed. "Yes, much better. Perhaps fae magic is good for more than glamours after all? Or is this just a particularly convincing glamour?" I try to laugh. It comes out sounding horrible.

Lodírhal rises slowly, wordlessly, and takes a few steps back. I cannot bring myself to lift my gaze, to discover if he's still looking at me. I stand as well, carefully stepping back behind the root on which I sat. One-shoed as I am, I move awkwardly but no longer limp.

"Gracious gods, how tired I am." I wrap my cloak tightly around my body. "I think I'll just shut my eyes for a little. You said you'll keep watch?"

He grunts. He seems about to say more, but I don't wait to hear it. I'm already retreating, stumbling over roots until I reach the far side of the oak. There I curl up, my head cradled on the crook of my arm, my legs curled beneath the folds of my cloak. I pull my hood over my face and squeeze my eyes shut.

But I cannot shut my ears. I lie there for what feels like hours, listening to the sound of Lodírhal's footsteps as he paces to and fro on the other side of the tree.

LODÍRHAL

"*B*ehind you!*"

I feel rather than see the huge, coiled limb lashing straight for my head. I'm quick enough to duck beneath it and narrowly avoid a bludgeoning, but a second tentacle snakes around my ankle and, with a sharp twist, pulls me off my feet. I hit the boards of the flat-bottomed barge hard, momentarily stunned.

And in that moment, a third tentacle slithers around my throat.

I have just enough time to cry out and grab hold with both hands before I'm lifted off my feet. I dangle in that coiling grasp as the whole barge sways wildly under the weight of the creature climbing up its stern. I thrash and kick uselessly even as the tentacle turns me around and I'm faced with a wide leering mouth full of too many rows of teeth. Lidless red eyes stare mercilessly into my own.

Suddenly, there's a reverberating *smack*.

The ugly head turns sharply to one side, spitting out a

stream of poisonous slime. The tentacle around my throat loosens, and I squirm free, dropping heavily to the boards. I look up and see the Miphata on my right, still holding the oar she's just used as a club. The momentum of her swing has unbalanced her, and she struggles to regain her footing as the barge sways. I stretch out a hand toward her—

A swarm of tentacles fills my vision.

Choking back a strangled cry, I whip my knife free of its sheath. The blade of pure *virmaer* steel slices cleanly through one slimy appendage. A gurgling shriek rips at my ears, but I lunge forward without pause, slashing through the flailing coils until I reach the gaping mouth.

I drive my knife straight back into the creature's throat, my arm disappearing into its jaws up to the elbow.

The monster gives one horrific bellow, belching a stink of rotten fish into my face, then falls back into the rushing river with a splash. Many tentacles trail along the barge boards and one after another slip into the dark water. But the very last of them holds on for an instant longer than the rest and gives the barge a mighty shove.

The already unstable river craft twists wildly to one side.

Hearing a yelp, I whip my head around just in time to see the Miphata pitch over the low side of the barge and into the rushing water.

For the space of a single heartbeat, I stare into that empty space where she should be.

The barge is moving . . . carried on by the rapid current . . .

I'm going to lose her.

In two strides, I cross the barge. The next instant, I plunge over the side into dark water. Cold closes over my head, and the current's swift pull instantly catches me, stronger than I'd expected. I fight it with every ounce of strength I possess. A few powerful kicks, and I break the surface to draw a deep breath into my lungs. Then, letting the flow carry me along, I turn to search for the girl. Where is she? She should have surfaced by now. Does she know how to swim?

A swish of fabric draws my eye. I dive and pull myself through the water, kicking as hard as I can. I try to keep my eyes open, but all is a churning chaos of froth and bubbles. My hands stretch out before me, searching, desperate.

My fingers close around a handful of cloth.

Once again I kick for the surface, which seems farther away this time. I breach it at last, surging up with a great gasp. The armful of cloth I hold tries to drag me down, but I wrestle against the river's strength, refusing to give in, refusing to be dragged back down, refusing to let go.

A small hand appears through the foam. I grasp it and yank the Miphata up. She breaks the water's surface, her eyes shut, her mouth gaping, and I hear her choke, struggling to catch a breath. Then, to my relief, she lets out a feeble cry. She couldn't do that if she weren't breathing.

"Don't fight me," I bark even as she begins to flail her arms.

She must hear me, for she responds to the command in my voice. Her flailing ceases, and she goes limp in my grasp. I wrap one arm across her chest and shoulders, pulling her close to me as I angle back, making myself as buoyant as possible. The current has us firmly in its hold now, and I cannot resist it while simultaneously keeping her head above water.

Then I see it: a fallen tree stretched out from the shore. I have just strength enough to kick us to one side so that the river pulls us straight into the branches. They scratch at every exposed bit of skin, yet I'm able to catch hold. I fear a tentacle will encircle my leg at any moment and drag me under. But it seems our attacker has given up on us two particularly resistant snacks.

I haul us along the tree, still working against the current. She turns in my grasp, and I say, "Can you grab hold?"

"Yes!" she sputters and reaches up a shaking hand. I see her fingers wrap tight, but I'm afraid to let her go; her fingers might be too weak after the shock of the cold river to keep a firm grip. She catches my eye. "I'm all right. Let's go."

"Make for the shore," I urge.

Together we sidle along the length of the tree, and surprisingly soon I discover firm footing. I brace both feet on river stones, then reach back to take hold of the Miphata's arm. She releases her hold on the tree and leans into me instead, nearly toppling us both into the shallows. But I manage to keep my balance, and we stagger up the muddy bank and collapse on dry land. The girl hacks and coughs, spitting up more water. I roll onto my back and stare up at the sky, breathing hard and waiting for my racing heart to slow.

"What was that thing?" the girl asks once her coughing spasm has passed.

"A grindylow," I respond. "Biggest I've ever seen." A shudder races down my spine. "Nasty devils."

"What happened to our boatman?"

I shrug. I'm fairly certain the boatman now resides in the grindylow's stomach. Or one of its stomachs. "Perhaps he got away?" I suggest, swiveling my gaze sideways to look at the Miphata.

Wet hair plasters her face, and bits of mud and leaves cling to her cheeks and forehead. She glares at me as water drips from her lashes. "You should have tried to save him," she says, then spits bits of muddy grass out of her mouth. A piece clings to her lip, and I find myself wanting to reach out and pluck it away . . . to smooth my thumb across that plump softness . . .

I growl and sit up instead, then rise to my feet and shake water from my long hair. "I don't know why you bother to care," I say, looking down my nose at the girl as she pushes onto her elbows. "Our boatman would have eaten us too, given the chance. I'm quite certain he planned to attempt it the moment we reached our destination and completed our bargain."

The girl grumbles but offers no further argument. She may be soft-hearted to a fault, but she's not stupid. I offer a hand. She shakes her head and unsteadily scrambles to her feet. Her sodden clothes cling to her body, emphasizing every curve and contour.

I realize I'm staring and quickly turn my gaze up the river. "We won't make it to Elishor Pass by sundown, I fear." I carefully keep my voice cold and dispassionate.

"We may as well make camp for the night. I'll get a fire going, and we'll dry your clothes."

"My clothes?" Though I don't look at her directly, I see the Miphata wrap her arms around her slim body. She's starting to shiver. "Um . . ."

"Yes," I answer shortly and, turning my back to the river, stride inland. Along the way I gather dry sticks into a bundle, swiftly accumulating an armload.

"Where are we, do you think?" the girl asks after trailing behind me in silence for some minutes.

"The Itylarra countryside," I answer. "It's tame enough so long as you avoid the rivers. I spent time here in my youth. We'll be safe for the night."

Which, in truth, surprises me. By and large, the ward witch's directions have led us through one deadly location after another. We progressed from the Goran Desolation to the Bridge of Caibalar, where only the Miphata's quick-witted answer to a riddle got us past a bloodthirsty troll. The following day, we were obliged to scale Mount Jofin before sunset or risk being devoured by mountain giants.

And just yesterday, we dined at the table of the Stone-Eyed Qisandoral—a demon of the First Age, much reduced in power but still potent in malice. We survived the poisonous feast, stole a golden apple from the demon's gardens, and made our way to the River Hycis, where we used the apple to bribe a boatman to carry us to the Elishor Pass.

Hopefully, the boatman enjoyed the forbidden fruit before meeting his slimy tentacled fate.

Now, five days into our journey, it's difficult to accept

the serenity of the landscape stretched out before us. But Itylarra is indeed one of the most heavenly valleys in all Eledria. My mother had a summer palace here and often brought me along with her when I was small, several centuries ago. The treacherous rivers serve to keep out more deadly predators, and the beings native to the valley are peaceful in nature. The air is richly perfumed with the scent of growing things.

Strange, that the ward witch would send us through Itylarra on our way to the Sundering Place. Then again, she probably thought we'd be dead long before now.

A brisk wind rustles through the grasses and graceful silver-branch trees. Behind me, I hear the Miphata's teeth start to chatter. "Do you think that . . . that *grindylow* counts as today's peril?" she asks. I cast a quizzical glance back over my shoulder, and she makes a face. "You know —seven days, seven nights, and seven perils. This is day five, so was that our fifth peril?"

"I rather hope so," I reply. "If not, I shudder to imagine what worse peril awaits us before the day's end."

She huffs a teeth-clattering laugh. By now we've reached a sheltered place above a grassy down. Not far off I see the antlered heads of peacefully grazing syv deer, each no more than twelve inches tall. Their burnished-gold coats glow gently as the sun begins to set and the world turns toward evening.

"Here," I say, dropping my bundle of collected fire-wood and kindling. "We'll stop here for the night."

The girl doesn't protest. She tries to help me light the fire, but I wave her off, for by this time she's trembling much too hard to be of any use. She finds a grassy knoll to sit on and huddles in a miserable bundle, watching me. From the corner of my eye, I see her touch the little respenia blossom, which somehow, miraculously, still clings to her hair. Alive, though by all odds it should have faded and died days ago.

The girl has a gift. Far beyond the range of her Miphates-trained powers. The spark of natural magic in her veins is undeniable. And terribly alluring.

I grimly shake off that thought and concentrate on the task at hand. After building a steeple of branches, I snap my fingers and set a spark to a pile of dried leaves and twigs. It takes a few attempts, but I soon get a lively blaze going. "There." I step back and run my fingers through my own damp hair. "Hang your garments from those branches, and they'll dry soon enough."

"Um . . ." She shoots me a sidelong glance. One of her shaking hands creeps to her collar. "And what will you . . .?"

I clear my throat, my forehead creasing into a frown. Focused on caring for her needs, I hadn't altogether thought this plan through. "The cold does not bother me, and my clothing will dry much faster than yours. I will . . . I will go about finding something for your evening meal."

She presses her lips together in a line. "Um, well . . . thank you."

I blink. And suddenly a hot rush floods my cheeks as I realize how foolish this is, how completely, irre-deemably idiotic. I am King Lodírhal of Aurelis, lord and master of the Dawn Court . . . now reduced to errand boy for a human mage girl? It's unnatural. Appalling.

Yet, when she lifts her lashes and those gray-blue eyes of hers meet mine . . . I fight the urge to smile.

"Have no fear, Miphata," I say. "You are safe in this place. I'll return anon."

With these words, I turn, intending to speed on my way. But something makes me stop and face her while I slip a hand inside my doublet. "Here." Taking a few quick strides toward her, I drop the carved-stone amulet and chain into her palm. "It's hardly sensible for me to carry this trinket when I cannot work the magic."

She gapes up at me. "But . . . but I thought . . ."

I don't want to hear whatever she has to say. I don't want to hear what she thought, however wrongly or rightly, about me. About her kidnapper. Without another word, I turn on my heel and stride off into the deepening twilight with the crackle of flames at my back. I feel her gaze on me until I've walked far across the grassy down, scattering syv deer along the way.

Gods above, what have I become? If anyone told me a mere five days ago that I would willingly hand over that amulet to my enemy . . . The very thought is laughable! And yet, what did I just do? Without a thought. Acting on an impulse I could resist no more than the inclination to breathe.

She shall strengthen every weakness . . . and weaken every strength . . .

How accurate are those prophetic words. How just, how apt. And how terrible.

Five days into this journey. Tonight, tomorrow, the next night—then, come dawn of the seventh day, we will arrive at the Sundering Place. And everything I've suffered on this journey will prove worthwhile the instant I break this bond, the moment I know myself to be free of her, free of this vicious hold she exerts over me.

Free ... free ...

"But maybe I don't *want* to be free?" I growl, tipping my head to snarl at the distant stars in a purpling sky. My voice rolls from my tongue and away, up into that endless arc. And I stand, head back, staring up and up.

I close my eyes.

I breathe deeply of all the perfumes this valley has to offer.

This place of gentle nature and nurturing is made for a girl like the Miphata—an Olorie mage with her love of growing things. She could be happy here. I would build her a house, and she could plant a garden. She could explore the scope of her magic, which the Miphates stripped from her when they made her Ilestriesa's vessel. She could become whole.

And I? I would require nothing from her. Certainly not. This binding was not of her choosing. I would receive nothing from her that she does not willingly give. Perhaps, for a little while at least, I might lay down my sword and spend my time fetching and carrying for her. Providing for her needs, her comforts, as her faithful servant-king.

A foolish fantasy. One I should never indulge.

Yet here I stand like a gods-blighted idiot with my eyes closed, while the whole dreamy, hazy picture plays out in my mind like a well-told tale.

Something tickles my nose.

I sniff, frown. Open one eye.

A scent hovers in the air, I scent that I recognize: *respenia*.

Briefly I wonder if the Miphata has followed me. But no, her little blossom has faded too much to generate this powerful an aroma.

I open my other eye and turn slowly in place while a smile tilts the corners of my mouth.

DASYRA

"*T*here, there, sweet one. Stay alive. Stay alive a little longer."

At the sound of my voice, the respenia in my fingers tries to lift its browning face, but the little blossom is fading fast. I don't know how it's lasted this long.

Sniffing, I shake off the stray tear trailing down my cheek while I carefully cup the blossom in my hands and press it close to my heart. I will it to receive some of my own lifeforce, but it lacks the strength to even try.

I don't think it will survive the night.

A breeze picks up and blows against my damp small clothes and exposed skin. I sit as close to the fire as I dare, angled to protect the flower from its heat. My gown, shift, and cloak hang from the tree branches overhead, dripping into the fire, which sputters and twists under the patter of droplets. But Lodírhal's magic called the blaze into being; it won't easily be doused.

Lodírhal . . .

I gaze into the flames, holding my shivering blossom

125

close to my heart, and let my tired mind wander back to that moment when we lay on the riverbank, having just survived one more in a series of life-threatening episodes. The moment he gazed into my eyes, looking at me with . . . with *that* expression.

Can there be any truth to this whole Fatebinding nonsense? I dismissed it out of hand at first. Sure, some sort of connecting curse threads entwined between this dangerous fae king and me might necessitate this little journey of ours. But an actual Fated Love? That's nonsense. Isn't it? The stuff of sentimental ballads and nothing to do with real life. It simply isn't reasonable to believe that two hearts, two souls, might be inextricably drawn to one another even before the moment of meeting. Called to voyage through life and love together by the inexorable will of destiny or fate or gods or eternity or . . .

I shake my head and squeeze my eyes shut, tucking in my chin. But even that's a mistake—for with my eyes closed, I can't seem to see anything but that look in his eye. The same look I've caught so many times over the last five days. A look that has the power to make my heart catch in my throat and my knees tremble and my stomach dip and plunge.

"Blight it all," I mutter, opening my eyes to stare up at distant stars slowly appearing through the branches and leaves overhead. The truth is—if I'm honest, brutally, painfully honest with myself—these past five days have been the best I've ever known. Frightening, yes. Punctuated by breathtaking thrills and near misses and pure blood-pounding terror. But so very . . . *full.* Full of life.

Full of excitement. Full of companionship as Lodírhal and I strove against the odds just to keep each other alive. Full of unity and connection such as I haven't known since . . . since . . .

Since the fae swept through my father's lands, destroying everything in their path.

A stone sinks in my gut. Here is the truth I must hold up against all other truths: The fae are the enemy. They always have been. They always will be. One or two potent *looks* from this undeniably charismatic and beautiful fae king changes nothing.

I bow my head again, biting my lips in the effort to suppress a welling sob. Which is stupid, so stupid. I am not this girl, ready to fawn and swoon and sigh with longing. It's just . . . it's just . . . it's just been so long since I felt as though I *belonged* anywhere.

But I do.

With Lodírhal . . . Though I don't want to admit it, though I don't want to feel it, with Lodírhal, I *do* belong.

Which is why I must finish this journey, face whatever perils remain, and get to the Sundering Place as soon as possible. Because this belonging, this bond is wrong. It's dangerous.

"You must get free," I whisper, trying to make myself hear, to make myself understand. "Free of *him*. Free of the Miphates. Free of all of them. Find your own place, stand on your own two feet."

Where will I go once the Sundering is complete? I let a blustering sigh escape my lips as I turn my gaze back to the fire. I've been unable to answer this question no matter how many times I turn it around in my head. I can't return to my own world. The Miphates will hunt me down. Ilestriesa is much too valuable a weapon. And the Warrior and I are bonded to the death. Would Mage Jhaan kill me to take back Ilestriesa and bind her to a more malleable Vessel? I wouldn't put it past him.

I shudder, one hand moving to touch the familiar weight of the amulet hanging between my breasts. Gods on high, I wish Lodírhal had kept it! Why did he give it back? Wasn't it supposed to be his means of manipulating me into complying with this journey? Why give it up?

Maybe he trusts me. Maybe he no longer fears I'll bolt at the first opportunity.

Maybe he realizes how deeply—how dangerously— I've begun to feel this Fatebinding too.

"Miphata?"

The sound of Lodírhal's voice ringing from the shadows beyond the firelight startles me. I open my mouth and begin to rise before realizing that I'm still wearing only my small clothes. Oh gods. Can he see me? All shivering and nearly naked?

"Just a moment," I call out and hastily press the respenia blossom back into my hair. Hands trembling, I snatch my still-damp shift from the nearest branch and haul it over my head. My skin shudders as the clammy fabric clings to my body, but it's better than nothing.

Straightening the skirt as best I can, I rise, wrap my arms around my middle, and gaze out beyond the shelter of the tree and the bright blaze. Evening has deepened significantly, and I struggle to make sense of the shadows. "Are you there, King Lodírhal?"

He appears, suddenly, as though by magic, entering the ring of firelight. His eyes are bright . . . too bright. Shining with some sort of feral magic.

He stops abruptly, and for a moment he does not move, does not breathe. His gaze fixes upon mine, and I feel the purposeful force with which he does not allow it to lower, to drink in the sight of my trembling, exposed body.

Heat rushes to my cheeks. "What . . . what have you got there?" I ask and jut my chin to indicate his hands, which are clasped strangely in front of his chest. "Something to eat, I hope?" I try to speak lightly, but my voice sounds a little shrill in my own ears.

He shakes his head. Then, without a word, he steps closer and opens his hands to display what rests in his palms.

It's a flower. An exquisite, shining blue flower with curling green tendrils gently searching along his palm and winding around his fingers. At the sound of my gasp, it turns its little blue face, its yellow center seeming to blink at me with sleepy disinterest.

"Respenia," I breathe and lift my gaze from the blossom to meet Lodírhal's golden eyes fixed so intently upon me. "How—? Where—?"

"I told you," he says, his voice a little rough at the edges. "I grew up in these parts. Respenia are rare, but they've been known to grow in this valley." He holds his hands a little closer to me. "Go on. Take it."

Fingers trembling, I place my hand near his, less than an inch away from the blossom. It sends out a green tendril to inspect my fingertip, my knuckle, my hand, like

129

a dog sniffing at a stranger. Then, as though reaching a decision, it wraps that tendril around my finger and climbs from Lodírhal's hand to mine. I can hardly breathe. My other hand quivering with excitement, I reach up to that place behind my ear where my own blossom still clings with the last of its strength. Carefully untangling it from strands of hair, I bring it down, holding my palms level.

Slowly the two flower heads turn to face one another —the one so bright, vibrant, and full of life, the other brown, faded, and nearly dead.

A moment of waiting. A painful hush.

Then, with a small buzzing purr, the fresh blossom crawls across the space between my hands, eagerly shooting out green stems to wrap around the frailer blossom and draw it into a close embrace. The buzzing increases, becoming an audible hum.

The fading blossom begins, ever so faintly . . . to shine.

I look at Lodírhal, who watches the meeting of the two respenia, his expression rapt. Sensing my gaze on him, he glances up at me, and I cannot stop the smile that bursts across my face. He blinks and takes a step back, averting his gaze.

With a hasty shake of my head, I turn from him and carry the two blossoms toward the tree trunk, to a little nesting place between its roots where the ground is soft and mossy. Kneeling, I set them down.

"They need earth," I say as I watch both blossoms shoot green tendrils into the ground and climb out of my hands. Together, they nestle into the moss. "They need to anchor themselves as they complete the bonding." Carefully, I slide my fingers out from under them.

"Will it work?" Lodírhal's voice asks from somewhere behind me. "Did we bring them together in time?"

I nod. "I think so." Chewing my lower lip, I sit back on my heels. "Only time will tell. By morning, I'll know for sure."

I turn to look back up at him. And there, in his eyes . . . that expression I've seen so many times in the last few days. Almost *hungry*. It takes my breath away. For a moment, I can't move. I feel as though all strength has drained from my limbs, leaving me weak before him. With an effort of will, I pull myself together, stand, and face him. Just holding his gaze takes everything I have.

"Are you happy?" he asks.

His need is acute, shining vividly from the depths of his soul. But . . . his need for what? For my pleasure? My delight? No, it can't be. He's a fae king, a merciless, ageless, terrible being. Our bond . . . or whatever you want to call it . . . it isn't real. It's the effect of capricious gods toying with us for their amusement. Surely whatever he feels is merely an outgrowth of this curse under which we both suffer.

But how can I deny that husky timbre in his voice? How can I pretend not to hear it?

"Yes," I whisper softly. And I realize that it's true. For the first time in I can't even say how long, I *am* happy. Foolishly, ridiculously, idiotically happy. Because, for the first time in such a long while, my happiness *matters* to someone.

An impulse takes hold. I don't know where it comes

from, but I respond without a thought. When I take a step toward him, he starts but doesn't retreat. He flinches but doesn't pull away as I place one hand on his chest. Rising on my toes, I lightly brush my lips against his cheek.

Something shocks through the air between us. So sharp, so strong, it makes me gasp.

I pull back, my hand still resting on his heart. I gaze into his eyes, which have widened until their golden irises are entirely ringed by white. Does he feel it too?

My heart throbs in my throat. I think it might choke me. Yet I cannot say whether it throbs with fear or . . . or something else.

I know only that a second impulse has taken hold of me. One I cannot ignore.

I lift my hand from his heart and place it on the side of his face. Moving more slowly, more cautiously this time, I rise on my toes again and press my lips to his cheek a second time, just at the corner of his mouth. I linger there a moment, my eyelashes fluttering softly.

His hand closes in a viselike grip around my wrist.

I sink back onto my heels and gaze up into his eyes. Gaze into a stare so hot, so deadly, I could melt beneath it. I should look away. But I can't. Gods help me, I can't.

Still holding tight to my wrist, he leans in, closing the distance between us. A gasp shudders from my throat, my lips parting, my gaze fixed on his mouth. But he stops. He remains poised there, just the barest fraction of space between us.

My heart thunders in my throat. I'm sure I hear his heart beating in counter-time.

A moment of perfect stillness hangs between us.

A moment of decision.

My decision.

I reach up with my free hand, catch him by the back of his head, and pull his mouth down to mine.

At first his lips are hard, unyielding. Then they soften, open, responding to my touch with a burst of such warmth and sweetness, my head feels light. A moan rumbles in his throat as he releases my wrist, cups my face with his hand, and turns his head, deepening the kiss. His other hand touches the nape of my neck, then his thumb trails down my spine, igniting sparks in one bone after another, making my back arch, my body mold to his.

At last, he presses his palm to the small of my back, and I feel the heat of his touch right through the thin, damp fabric of my shift. Closer and closer he draws me, until I'm sure I'll melt into him. My arms wrap around his neck as my lips drink in his. He takes a few steps, backing me up until my shoulders contact the tree trunk, and his kisses begin to wander from my mouth to my cheek, my jaw, down my neck. My skin burns at every touch, all fear, all hesitation forgotten.

Tangling my fingers in his golden hair, I pull his head back up and claim his mouth for another, longer, deeper kiss—

"Well, well, well. What do we have here?"

I choke on a cry, my eyes flying open. I feel a jolt shoot through Lodírhal's body as though he's just been pierced by an arrow between the shoulders. His arms tighten, and he draws back his head, gazing into my wide eyes.

Then slowly, carefully, he steps back. For a moment, I stand against the tree trunk, sheltered in the circle of his arms, his wide shoulders a barrier against the world. But it cannot last.

He turns.

And I see the ominous figure looming just on the other side of our fire.

"Kyriakos," Lodírhal says.

LODÍRHAL

"I heard rumor of the King of Aurelis traveling down the Hycis River with his stolen bride. Word of your many adventures has spread far and wide throughout Eledria. Like lovers from an ancient ballad, or so some say."

The Lord of Ninthalor's voice rolls like pure darkness over me, shrouding even the bright flames that had, only moments before, raged so hot in my heart and soul.

Gods blight! I grind my teeth, stopping the curse before it escapes in a vicious growl. I'd hoped to keep this whole affair secret. The last thing I need is for word of my current vulnerability to reach my enemies' ears. Though I'm not certain I possess a single enemy more deadly than the friend standing across the fire from me now.

I square off, planting myself in front of the Miphata as though I might turn myself into a living wall. A mistake, I realize—for Kyriakos takes note of the protective impulse and my inability to suppress it. He smiles, his teeth flashing, and his eyes, flickering in the firelight, meet mine.

My hands slowly curl into fists. "And who might have initiated these tales?" I ask, my voice liquid and calm. It fools no one, least of all Kyriakos. But this is how the game is played. And we are both master players.

"Who can say?" Kyriakos answers with an easy shrug. "The stream runs to the river, the river to the sea, yet the source of all remains a mystery." He steps around the fire, lifting one hand to gently brush aside the Miphata's suspended and still-dripping gown. He pauses a moment to inspect the gown, then looks my way again, raising an eyebrow. "Tell me, good king, have you found it necessary to resort to more . . . *aggressive* persuasions to keep your little Fatebonded by your side? Or does the charming scene I just witnessed bode ill for the completion of your journey?"

I know what he's asking. Our bargain: Is it still good? And if not . . .

I don't want to answer. But to remain silent will reveal too much. Besides, when all is said and done, when all the facts are aligned and inspected with a rational eye, only one answer can be given.

I open my mouth.

Before a single word can cross my lips, a shoulder jostles my arm. I look down but am too late to prevent the Miphata from stepping boldly out in front of me. Though she wears only her thin shift, she stands with the regal posture of a queen, her arms crossed over her danger-ously exposed bosom, her chin lifted, her shoulders back. She might as well be clad in the full regalia of her order.

"All right," she says, her voice crisp and bold. "I've had about enough of this secretive back-and-forth between the two of you in your fae tongue. You are both perfectly capable of making yourselves understood by human ears. If you have anything further to say, you will include me. That, or take yourselves away and complete your little conference elsewhere."

Kyriakos's gaze slowly travels from me to the girl. It's a lingering, languid, indulgent sort of gaze. A gaze without haste or embarrassment. I watch his eyes rove from the tumble of dark curls around her face to the loose ties of her low-cut garment over her bosom. I see him noting how the damp fabric clings to her every curve. He might as well be undressing her right in front of me.

Even worse, I sense the glamour emanating from him. A glamour most subtle and profound. I know only too well the fascination Kyriakos holds for human women. Never, for as long as I've known him, has he failed to bring about a desired conquest.

I want to step in the way. I long to block that glamour, block that gaze. I want to launch myself across the fire, wrap my hands around his throat, and throttle him until he's choking in the dirt at my feet.

But if I do, I'll be playing into Kyriakos's hand.

She shall strengthen every weakness . . . and weaken every strength . . .

I clench my teeth and grimly stand my ground.

The Miphata, however, draws a short, sharp breath through her nostrils and takes a half step back. Then, with a quick flick of her wrist, she waves aside the glamour spell reaching out to her as easily as she might swat a fly. It's such a swift, deft motion, I almost miss it. But the effect is immediate. The simmering tension in the air dissipates, replaced by something else. Something even more sinister.

Kyriakos smiles. "Well, Lodírhal." He allows the magic in his voice to alter the shape of his words, making them comprehensible even to those who do not know the language. "She is certainly an impressive little specimen of humanity. But then, one should expect no less from the Vessel of Ilestriesa."

His gaze drops again to the girl's bosom and to the stone amulet resting between her breasts; the next instant, it cuts to meet mine like the slash of a knife. I clearly hear his unspoken words: *We had an agreement, Lodírhal. Or have you forgotten?*

Before I can think of a response, Kyriakos turns from me again and sweeps an elegant bow. "Pardon my discourtesy, most illustrious Miphata. I certainly would not wish to offend so fair a lady. In fact, quite the opposite. Upon hearing word of your presence in Itylarra, I altered my own course of travel that I might offer you and my good friend Lodírhal an evening's hospitality."

"An evening's hospitality?" she echoes, narrowing her eyes. "And who are you exactly?"

He places a hand over his heart. "Kyriakos of Ninthalor, Lord of Noxaur and servant of King Beldroth. I am lately come from the wars in Seryth, taking the long way back to my homeland, enjoying the many fair sights Eledria has to offer. My party waits just yonder, over the hill. We have food and wine aplenty. The two of you have traveled hard these last five days, or so I understand, and greater trials are yet to come. Why not take your ease for a moment? Indeed, lovely human, you must be hungry.

Unless . . ." He flicks another glance my way. "Unless of course your appetite runs to different sustenance than spiced fruits and sweet breads."

I hold his gaze and begin, "We thank you for the generosity of your offer, Lord Kyriakos—"

In that moment, a terrible grumbling growl interrupts. The Miphata lets out a yelp of surprise, flattens one hand over her stomach, and looks up at me, her face flushing a bright crimson. "I, um . . . I'm so sorry. He said spiced fruits and sweet breads, and I suddenly realized just how hungry I am. We've had little to eat these last few days . . ." Her voice trails off, and her eyes gaze up at me with gentle pleading.

I want to snarl. I want to growl and curse and tell her not to be a fool. Sitting down to a meal with Kyriakos of Ninthalor can be nothing short of hazardous. But how can I protest in the face of her altogether human need?

"You need not worry, Lodírhal, my old friend," Kyriakos continues, his voice an easy purr. "No bargains necessary. My offer is genuine and made with an open hand. Come! If you feel you must repay me, you may fill in some of the gaps in my knowledge of your little quest. It's a tale well worth the hearing, by all accounts."

The Miphata lowers her head, but I hear her stomach utter another unmistakable growl. It's so loud, so impossible to ignore, I almost wonder if Kyriakos managed to get a spell through her defenses after all, to make her feel this hunger. But I don't sense his magic on her.

"Very well," I say, answering my old friend's smile with one of my own. "We shall indeed be glad of a respite tonight."

Kyriakos inclines his head. Then, with a single fluid, insidious gesture, he reaches up, snatches the Miphata's damp gown, and pulls it free of the branch. He hands it to her, even as his gaze once more rakes across her figure.

This time, I don't stop and think. I let my instinct respond to the impulse of the moment and step in front of the girl, blocking her from his view. His smile falters, fades. His brow lowers, and his eyes meet mine, hard. I do not break that gaze.

"I'll, um . . ." The Miphata clears her throat. "I'll just step around behind the tree and change, shall I?"

DASYRA

*M*y heart pounds. Thundering in my ears.

I can't say whether it's the arrival of this wholly unsettling Lord Kyriakos that has set my pulse to racing or . . . maybe the fault lies with those kisses I still feel burning on my lips, my jaw, my neck . . . the memory of strong warm hands pressing my body closer, closer . . .

Oh gods! How easily I fell into Lodírhal's embrace. How readily I would have fallen deeper still, heedless of all consequences.

The air is colder on this side of the silver-branch tree, away from the fire. I shiver as I slip into my gown and cringe as the clammy fabric envelops me. Still, unpleasant though it may be, it effectively douses the heat in my veins. One can hardly dwell on remembered kisses while every step, every movement means damp squelching. My stomach growls again. I snort and begin lacing up the side of my bodice. The arrival of that Noxaurian fae was a good thing, really. One should never make impulsive and potentially life-altering decisions on an empty stomach.

Though, in the moment when his lips hovered so close to mine . . . when I felt the heat of his desire scorching the small slice of air between us . . . it didn't feel like a decision. It felt like inevitability.

Fate.

"Gods-blighted Fatebond," I muttered, securing the last lace. With a quick shake of my head, I push loose hair off my face. This is ridiculous. I have a good head on my shoulders and both feet firmly back on the ground. I will march out there and face those two fae like nothing untoward has happened.

Like the one hadn't just caught me pressed up against the trunk of a tree with my arms wrapped around the neck of the other.

"Gods save me," I whisper, pressing my hands to my burning cheeks. Then, squaring my shoulders and lifting the edge of my damp skirts, I force my feet into motion and round the trunk of the silver-branch tree, my head high, my expression a calm mask. Time to show these fellows I can play fae games of inscrutability with the best of them.

Lodírhal and Kyriakos are still exchanging rumbling growls like a couple of posturing tomcats. I ignore them to crouch among the tree roots where a faint glow of blue glimmers in the shadows. The two respenia blossoms clasp each other close, the one bright and confident, the other faint but slowly gaining strength. I smile as I gaze down at them.

Then my smile melts into a frown. I want to take them

with me, but to disturb them now might cause irreparable damage. They must complete the bond to be safe.

Well, this Kyriakos fellow did say his camp is just over the hill, right? Surely I can return to this spot come dawn and fetch my blossoms before Lodírhal and I continue on our way ... on our way to ...

On our way to the Sundering Place.

A shiver races down my spine. I wrap my arms around my middle and rise, my head bowed. I can't quite find the will to turn and face the two fae, who have quieted and now watch me closely. But I can't stand here forever, can I?

I lift my chin, force a tight smile into place, and turn around. Lodírhal immediately catches my eye, his gaze questioning. Concerned? I offer a short nod. "They're fine," I say, assuming the question and offering an answer. "They'll be ready for travel come morning." Next, I address myself to Kyriakos, my voice crisp and clear. "Shall we, then?"

The Noxaurian fae's black eyes glitter in the firelight. He sweeps a graceful bow without bothering to hide the sardonic tilt of his lips. Every move and gesture this man makes is pure poison, I'm certain of it. But when he turns and sets out across the valley, I fall into step behind him.

Lodírhal quickly draws alongside me, and I get the distinct impression he intends to speak. What will he say? What can he say? What do I *want* him to say? I don't know. And suddenly I'm afraid ... afraid of this ageless, beautiful being who just stole my breath away with his kisses and who ... who ...

Who may have stolen my heart as well.

But does he want it? My heart?

The answer should be clear enough. He has fought tooth and nail to get us to the Sundering Place. To end this bond between us. Of course, he doesn't want my heart. He doesn't want me. How could he?

Except . . . maybe . . .

"Miphata," he begins, his low voice rumbling in my gut.

I pick up the edge of my skirts and quicken my pace, swiftly putting distance between us. Whatever he wants to say, I'm quite sure I'm not ready to hear it.

THE MOON IS high overhead by the time we reach the Noxaurian camp. I cannot gain a solid impression of how big the camp is, of how many people are gathered in the space. They've hung up eerie lanterns that cast a pale white glow, and by that glow I glimpse only flickering impressions of shapes, all wafting and graceful and unconsciously dangerous. The movements evoke a sense of choreography, as though, instead of a meal being prepared and served, I observe the performance of a sacred dance.

But then I see the meal. And all other impressions fade.

The food is arranged like a picnic across beautiful woven blankets spread over the ground. Aromatic breads, somehow warm and steaming, though where our hosts could have found baking ovens in this middle of this valley, I cannot guess. Sugared fruits glitter in the glowing lanterns like gems. Spiced meats, fishes . . . There are so many intoxicating smells that it's all I can do in my near-ravenous state to not dive headlong into one of those dishes like a pig to the trough.

Somehow, I manage to maintain my decorum and follow Kyriakos to the blanket he chooses, spread beneath a cluster of three slim trees with leaves shaped like crescent moons. He sprawls, stretching his body like a cat, his torso propped up on one elbow. The front of his robes opens to reveal an expanse of well-muscled chest, and his dark hair wafts across his shoulders and brushes the ground. Perfectly aware of the picture he makes, he casts me a sharp-eyed glance to see if I've noticed. But I'm far more interested in the food just now.

Lodírhal sits across from Kyriakos, equally graceful but more upright and dignified. I'm left to take a place between them, perching uncomfortably on my knees and heels, unable to relax in this strange atmosphere.

A shadowy form, not quite visible, hands me a goblet. As I start to lift it to my lips, Lodírhal reaches out and places his hand over the top. I meet his gaze, and he shakes his head slowly. Well, best not then. I set the goblet aside, casting an uneasy glance Kyriakos's way. The dark fae lord pops purple berries into his mouth one after another and doesn't acknowledge me.

When the shadowy servants offer me bread and spicy-smelling dipping sauce, I turn to Lodírhal, afraid he will again warn me away. This time, however, he nods, so I begin to eat . . . and discover quite suddenly just how ravenous I am. It's been far too long since I ate a proper meal. Lodírhal has done his best to provide for my needs, but as he himself requires so little sustenance, I don't think he quite realizes the scope of human appetites.

I'm uncomfortably aware of his scrutiny as I tuck into the bread, along with every drop of sauce in its dainty bowl, then an assortment of sugared fruits, and finally a great haunch of slow-roasted meat from some animal I don't recognize, so mouthwateringly soft and juicy that I can't stop myself from taking bite after bite, even long after my stomach is swollen.

At last I sit back, unable to bear another mouthful . . . and only then realize how parched I am. Kyriakos and Lodírhal are quietly eating with far less gusto than I just displayed. Occasionally, our host asks a question in his strange fae language. Lodírhal offers terse replies between bites.

I settle down a little more comfortably, one hand resting on my tight stomach. I'm suddenly aware of many eyes watching me covertly from all sides. But when I turn my head, I can never quite catch any of the watchers. I see only more shadows flitting between the globe lanterns. All silent and serene.

"So, Miphata." Kyriakos's voice draws my attention back to his lounging form. "I am simply agog to learn more details of this adventure you've been living. Tell me, is it true that you manifested the Warrior Spirit and slew a wild-magic being in the Goran Desolation?"

Suddenly, I wish I'd not eaten quite so well. My stomach turns over, and I tuck my chin, grimacing. The last thing I want is to tell the story of my first kill like . . .

like it's some sort of ballad or minstrel's tale. The experience was not something I want to relive.

"The Miphata has proven herself a worthy ally on this journey," Lodírhal's voice interposes, filling my silence. "Where need arises, she does what she must."

"High praise indeed, coming from a human-hater such as yourself," Kyriakos says with another of his flashing grins.

Human-hater? I try to glance Lodírhal's way but find myself suddenly incapable of doing so. My stomach churns again. Was the food ensorcelled after all?

Kyriakos sits up suddenly, crossing his legs and resting his elbows on his knees. "As you are so unwilling to elaborate on the adventures you've already had, tell me this instead: Did my little friend give you any idea what your final peril will be once you reach the Sundering Place?"

Little friend? I blink. Does he mean the ward witch? I seem to remember the name "Kyriakos" coming up between the witch and Lodírhal during that strange meeting.

I also remember the young witch's swelling belly . . . and the look in her eye when she spoke her last words to me: *"Get yourself unbound and free before you find you don't want to be free anymore."*

"She did not," Lodírhal says, answering the question after an extended silence. "Each peril we faced has proven a unique surprise. But the Miphata and I handled them with ease, and I expect nothing different regarding whatever lies ahead."

Kyriakos raises one dark brow. "You two make a formidable team."

Lodírhal sips his wine. The same wine, I note, that he would not let me drink. Gods on high, I'm truly parched! My throat feels as though it will close right up with dryness.

Drawing a quick, determined breath, I stand and brush off my skirts. Lodírhal, startled, hastily rises as well, while Kyriakos merely tilts his head, looking lazily up at me. "Don't worry," I say quickly, not quite meeting Lodírhal's eye. "I simply need to . . . um . . . answer a call of nature. If you'll grant me privacy, good lords, I'll return shortly."

Lodírhal looks momentarily confused. Then understanding dawns, and he blinks, embarrassed. Such "calls of nature" never seem to be an issue for the fae, at least not that I've noticed. "Very well, Miphata," he says. "Be careful. Don't go far."

"Didn't you say this valley is safe?"

"It is, yes. But don't venture down to the river's edge."

"I hardly think I'll be going that far," I answer lightly. With that, I slip away from our little picnic tableau, glad of an excuse to put distance between myself and both of my companions. I have an odd feeling that many eyes watch me as I go, but when I look back, I see no one.

I make my way into a nearby stand of trees—more of those trees with the crescent-shaped leaves that seem to catch the moonlight overhead and offer it back in a gentle glow, making it possible for even my human eyes to see in the darkness. I find a private enough spot to accomplish the very human task at hand . . . but when I'm through, I feel reluctant to return to the feast. My stomach still feels uncomfortably tight, and my throat is dry as a bone.

Suddenly, a sound tickles my ear—gurgling. A stream? Lodírhal warned me against rivers, but he said nothing about a stream. And though part of me knows I should return to him at once, my thirst is becoming harder to ignore.

With a frustrated huff of air, I turn to follow the sound of water and soon discover a brook babbling cheerfully among the glowing trees. "Thank the gods for small blessings!" I whisper and kneel on the bank, scooping a handful of water before I even stop to consider. It's cool and delicious on my lips, and the moment it passes over my tongue and down my throat, I feel an immediate flood of relief and refreshment. A flood so profound . . . it feels like a spell.

No, I take that back. It *is* a spell.

Gods blight it! How could I have been so careless? How many times have I been told stories of unwary lads and lasses drinking from Faerieland streams? How can I hope to survive in this world on my own if I can't even remember such simple lessons?

On my own.

On my own.

A weight descends upon me, bowing my shoulders, bowing my spirit.

We will reach the Sundering Place the dawn after tomorrow. So soon. So terribly soon. After that, the binding will be broken, and Lodírhal and I will part ways. Forever. Unless . . .

Oh, blight and blast that Kyriakos! If only I could get

Lodírhal alone. If only I could speak to him, find out what he's honestly thinking behind that impenetrable mask of glamour he wears. Because that kiss—all those kisses—they didn't feel like the kisses of a man determined to break this bond.

I rise, sway a little, and almost stagger into the stream. Catching my balance, I turn and start to make my way back toward the camp. The spell bubbles in my veins, forcing me to stop and lean against tree trunks every few paces. And those Noxaurians are so wretchedly quiet.

Without a breath of sound to guide my way, I can scarcely find my way back to the encampment. But I glimpse a glowing white orb light flashing through the leaves and branches, and I turn my unsteady footsteps that way.

"I trust you've not forgotten our bargain, my friend."

I start at the abrupt break in the silence. That's Kyriakos's voice, dark and deep as a midnight sky. Why does he now speak in a language I can understand? Especially since I am not, as far as he knows, present to hear it.

Lodírhal responds in kind, his voice a bright, golden contrast to the Noxaurian lord's. "I have not forgotten."

"To have come this far," Kyriakos continues, "to have endured so much . . . it would be a shame not to see it through now."

"And whose fault is it that the journey has not been as straightforward as I initially anticipated?"

"What? You don't appreciate the little adventures spun for you by my pretty witch friend? Don't look at me so. I may have offered her a suggestion or two, but she is a most inventive creature and, for a human, surprisingly well traveled through Wanfriel. Besides, she's yet to throw anything your way that you and the young Miphata did not handle with aplomb. So, tell me, Lodírhal, do you find your resolve weakening?"

"When have you ever known my resolve to weaken, Kyriakos?"

"Never. But then, neither have I discovered you locked in passionate embrace with a human maid before. That, I must say, took me quite by surprise. And certainly made me wonder as to the outcome of our bargain."

"It's none of your business."

"I beg to differ. Our bargain is very much my business. And if I see the outcome threatened—"

"You're more than willing to offer counter-threats."

"Perhaps."

There's a pause. My head spins. I'm obliged to rest my hand against the trunk of a tree just to keep myself upright. What is this that I'm hearing? It doesn't sound right, doesn't *feel* right. But I can't stop up my ears now. I've already heard too much.

Suddenly, Kyriakos speaks again in dark, dangerous tones: "Believe you me, my friend: If you do not spill her blood across the Sundering Stone and offer up her spirit to the goddess, if you do not hand over the amulet of Ilestriesa into my keeping, you will regret it. I will personally see to that."

My heart stops, lodged in my throat. I try to breathe. For a moment, I cannot.

Then, with a ragged gasp, I pull away from the tree and retreat several staggering paces into the forest.

A bargain . . .

Spill her blood . . .

Of course. Of course, it all makes sense. Perfect sense.

Lodírhal wants free of his Fatebond. A bond that makes him vulnerable, that could all too easily kill him. Kyriakos knew the way. And Kyriakos wants . . .

My hand flies to my breast, clutching the amulet hidden beneath my bodice. *Ilestriesa*. Kyriakos wants the Warrior. And he bargained my death in exchange for it.

I feel the throb of the stream spell moving in my limbs. But it's a distant sensation now, a dull ache beneath the fiery roar of fear and betrayal coursing through my soul.

Lodírhal . . . Would he . . .? Could he . . .?

I can't think, can't finish the question. Only one thought takes hold in my brain, dominating all else.

Run.

Run.

Run!

I turn and flee into the shadows.

LODÍRHAL

I swirl the wine in my cup, idly admiring how the moonlight plays on the dark liquid. Kyriakos watches me, his eyes narrowed and knowing. I pretend not to notice or care.

I also pretend that my attention isn't drawn toward the forest where the Miphata disappeared. Why has she not yet returned? How long does it take for humans to . . . do their necessary business? I'm not exactly familiar with their ways, but it's never taken her this long before.

With a sudden gusting sigh, Kyriakos lies back on the blanket, lacing his fingers behind his head and crossing one ankle over the opposite knee. Though I try not to look, my eyes flick his way and momentarily catch his gaze. A smile plays on his lips.

Suppressing a growl, I lift my cup and take a quick gulp, then wipe my mouth with the back of my hand and turn away. Kyriakos's threats still echo in my ear: *If you do not spill her blood across the Sundering Stone and offer up her spirit to the goddess . . . If you do not hand over the amulet of Ilestriesa into my keeping . . .*

My jaw hardens. I try to tell myself that I care nothing for his empty talk. The Lord of Ninthalor is powerful, to be sure, but his power doesn't come close to equaling mine. He can mutter and posture all he likes; there's little he can do. Besides, our bargain was conditional: I only owe the amulet if I successfully break the Fatebond. If not . . .

If not . . .

I take another sip of wine.

Strange. Strange, how awareness of the truth comes to one so slowly and yet, in a way, has always been known. Unacknowledged, perhaps, but known.

I must acknowledge it now. I must face the truth that's been growing in my heart for days now. There's no point in resisting. Not anymore.

I have no intention of performing the Sundering.

Gods on high! Is it truly so simple? But, of course, it is. I've continued this weary journey day after weary day merely as an excuse to remain close to the Miphata. The end goal, now so perilously near . . . it no longer matters to me.

I would rather die than spill her blood.

But how will she respond when I tell her we won't be finishing the journey? What if she insists that we must? She does not know the doom in store for her once we reach the Sundering Place. She does not know that for the Fatebond to be broken, one of us must die. What if she asks? What if she insists?

What will she say when I admit that I knew all along the sacrifice required?

She'll hate me. How could she not? I've tricked her, deceived her. Betrayed her in my heart. She will look into my eyes and see what a selfish monster I am. I cannot bear that.

Frowning, I take another gulp of wine, rolling the spicy sweetness around on my tongue as I consider my options. Why take such a dire view of things? After all, I might never need to tell her the truth. That kiss under the silver-branch tree . . . that kiss was revealing. I had used no glamour on her, devised no trickery. When she reached out to me, when she touched my cheek with her lips, it was entirely her own idea.

And when she closed the space between our lips and sealed my kiss with hers . . . she wanted it. She wanted it as urgently as I did. Which means she must feel something for me. She must.

There's a chance . . .

I shake my head and smile with only the faintest trace of bitterness. I never imagined I'd find myself in such a predicament. Find myself hoping, desperately hoping, to be bound for all eternity to a human.

But then, I've never known a woman like her before. With her gentle strength, her courage. Her mercy. Her kindness. All my life I've been surrounded by the glamours and subtle arts of the fae courts. But *she* is so true. True and honest and forthright in her very being. To be in her presence is to draw fresh air into my lungs for the very first time. And after that first breath, how could I return to the stagnant suffocation of my previous existence? How could I bear it?

I'm in love. Gods help me.

"She shall strengthen every weakness . . . weaken every strength." The words slip through my lips in a whisper. And I smile.

Then I rise. I won't wait a moment longer. I must find her, confront her. Tell her what is in my heart. I will not hide anymore.

Kyriakos turns his head to gaze up at me. A lazy smirk still curls his lips. "And where are you off to?"

I cast him a dismissive glance. "Good night, Kyriakos. Your hospitality is no longer—"

Pain shoots through my heart. I gasp, press a hand to my chest. After the first burst, the pain lessens, and I breathe out slowly.

Then it spikes again, sharper than before. Lights explode on the edges of my vision, and when I try to draw another breath, I cannot. My feet move as though wanting to outrun this attack. But I am dizzy, weak. My legs give out, and I collapse to my knees. Through an agonized haze, I'm just aware of Kyriakos smoothly rising to a seated position, resting his elbow on one upraised knee. He eyes me closely as I double over.

"What is this?" I snarl when the second spasm passes and I'm able to form coherent words. "What have you done to me?"

"I? Done to you?" Kyriakos finds his goblet and takes a delicate sip of wine. "You know me well enough to trust I wouldn't break the laws of hospitality. Not overtly, anyway."

Grimacing, I send my awareness inward, searching for some trace of spell or curse slipped through via food or drink. There is nothing. Another wave of pain takes me, and I choke and fall to my face. It is then, in that terrible moment of vulnerability, of agony, that I recognize the sensation. I've felt it before.

The Miphata. She's . . . she's gone. Slipping away from me, farther and farther. Straining the binding thread that connects us. Straining it until it constricts painfully around my heart, threatens to rip it in two. Can she not feel that pain herself?

But no. No, she isn't fae. She wouldn't feel it like I do, not this acutely.

The spasm passes. I tremble, weak with temporary relief. Then, with a growl, I push upright and turn on Kyriakos, my fists balled, my teeth gnashing. "Where is she?"

Kyriakos blinks innocently up at me. "How would I know? She's *your* Fatebonded."

"You did something to her."

"And break the laws of hospitality?" He takes another sip of wine, then casually wipes his hand across his lips. "I wouldn't dream of such a thing."

Turning from him, I stretch my awareness out along the cord of connection. Somewhere at the far end of it, I can just sense her. I try to send my voice out to her along that connection. But I don't know her name. I never learned it, never asked for fear she would refuse the offering. Without it, I cannot reach her.

And suddenly . . . she's gone.

Gone.

Passed beyond the bounds of this reality.

She must have found a gate. One that I taught her how to use. She has slipped from this world back into Wanfriel.

I collapse to my face again, shuddering as wave after wave of pain courses through me. It's a long while before I can feel anything else. When at last a hazy awareness breaks through, I find Kyriakos crouched beside me, one hand on my shoulder. His eyes glitter in the moonlight.

"You really did fall for her, didn't you?" He laughs cruelly. "I never thought to catch you so low. But I'm not one to miss an opportunity."

His hands roughly grip my arms and haul me upright. Holding me fast, he forces me to look into his eyes.

"Dawn is upon us, Lodírhal. The sixth day. And I, my friend, am your sixth peril." His voice is sharp, full of knives. "Now tell me: Do you want to save your Fatebonded's life?"

DASYRA

I hate to leave my respenia blossoms behind. But I dare not go back for them. That would mean passing too close to Kyriakos's camp. Besides, I cannot pull them up while they're bonding.

So, I must flee on my own through the shadows of this strange forest, putting as much distance between myself and Lodírhal as possible. Over the last five days, I've learned how to search for gates into Wanfriel. Finding one is probably my best bet. Once I'm through into the forest, I should be able to locate a Hinter path and travel swiftly across worlds, stepping through several realities before Lodírhal even realizes I'm gone.

He'll pursue, of course. The thought makes me tremble with dread. Is this how I'll spend the rest of my days? On the run from the man I'd dared to think I might . . . dared to think I could . . .

Growling, I push on through the trees, shoving low-hanging boughs out of my way. The spell throbs in my veins, making me dizzy. And beneath the throb, an ache around my heart grows more painful with every step I take. I ignore it and push on until I abruptly come upon a gate so small, I might easily have missed it—a delicate arch of spiderweb spread between two young silver-branch saplings. The gossamer strands glitter in the moonlight, and beneath them shimmers that strange distortion in the air that indicates a thin place in reality.

I stop, head throbbing, heart pounding, swaying heavily. Part of me longs to look back over my shoulder. To peer through the trees for some sign of Lodírhal.

No! I know better. I know the fae for what they are. Monsters and manipulators. Ravagers and destroyers. They are the enemy. And Lodírhal himself, did he not try to kill me at our first meeting? Can I ever forget the pressure of his arm around my neck, choking the life out of me?

He'll spill my blood. If I stand between him and what he wants, he won't even hesitate.

I circle the saplings twice in one direction, three times in the other, then duck swiftly beneath the spiderweb, careful not to brush it with the top of my head. I feel once more that chilling sensation of almost-pain ripple through me as I pass between realities.

Then I fall to my knees, my hands sinking into soft green grass. Daylight pools around me. I lift my head, bleary with the spell fog, and blink at my surroundings. I've left the night of the Itylarra Valley behind; I've come to the sixth day of my journey.

And is Lodírhal my sixth peril? Or was he the only real peril all along?

Shuddering, I drag myself to my feet and stagger into

the trees. The pain in my heart sharpens, coupled with the throb of the spell in my veins, until I'm hardly aware of anything else. Only pain. But Lodírhal will realize I've fled, and he'll be on my trail soon. I must put more distance between us, I must . . . I must . . . I can't even think. I can't do anything but force my body on, one step after another. I feel as though I'm swimming through a sea of anguish and fear, ready to sink, ready to drown.

Suddenly, an oak tree stands before me. Something inside me remembers: *Oaks are friendly to humans.* Desperate for any sort of relief, I stagger to its trunk and collapse amid a snarl of bulging roots. Faintly, ever so faintly, I sense protection around me. It isn't much, yet in that moment it's everything.

I press my cheek against the trunk, letting its rough bark dig into my skin. Tears fall. Or perhaps they've been falling all this time. I don't know. I don't care.

Lodírhal.

How could I have been so foolish? I believed he loved me. I truly believed . . . and I fell for his trickery. I followed at his heels, as trusting as a dog, while he led me to my death.

I've never been anything but a tool for other people's use.

Something hot burns my skin. I shift, uncomfortable. The heat rises, searing right through my misery. Is it more of the heart pain that increased with every step I took away from Lodírhal? But no, this is something else. A pain not of the soul but of the flesh.

The fabric of my bodice begins to smoke: The Warrior's amulet is scorching me. With a cry, I yank on the chain and pull the amulet out, away from my skin. As I hold it up before my eyes, it rotates slowly, the carved spell flashing in and out of my blurred vision.

Dasyra.

I frown. What is that? A voice in my head? A voice I don't know, and yet . . . it's strangely familiar.

Dasyra, summon me.

I scowl, feeling the ache in my heart deepen. Soon I'll be lost in it, unable to think or act. And the spell in my veins has only intensified since I stepped into Wanfriel.

Dasyra, hurry!

There's no ignoring a voice like that. Even as a subtle impression in the back of my mind, it's full of imperious authority. The voice of a commander.

Summon me now! Before we're both lost!

Desperately I close my fingers around the amulet. It burns into my palm, but I lean into that pain as a distraction from the worse pain in my soul. *"Tanatar, wynal-ha,"* I whisper. *"Anaerin, mir yinthana, abore so thula—Ilestriesa!"*

Magic responds to my summons, piercing the thin places between worlds, pouring through into the reality in which I sit. The oak tree sways and groans, and I can almost feel its roots tighten their hold to keep from being knocked over by the force of that magic flow. My eyes, blurred by enchantment, seem suddenly to sharpen, focus.

The Warrior appears.

That's strange. Always before she has manifested through me, her humble vessel. But this time she seems to stand in front of me—tall and gleaming, her dark skin and white hair somehow translucent, her eyes like gleaming jewels with inner fire. She looks down at me where I crouch with my back against the oak tree. One stern brow rises, and she slowly shakes her head and points at my wrist.

"See there," she says.

I look. And I gasp. Something is attached to my wrist: a spirit form not unlike the shining Ilestriesa, a spell resembling a snake wound round and round my forearm. Two sharp fangs sunk deep into my veins are pumping poison in bursts.

"Oh!" I gasp. In a horrifying way, it's funny: I knew the instant I drank from that stream that I'd ingested a spell, yet until this moment, when I see the spell for what it is, I simply could not comprehend my own danger. The spell's poison blocked my awareness. "Oh," I repeat, feeling small and foolish under Ilestriesa's knowing gaze.

The Warrior crouches before me. Her strong hand latches hold of the snake and, with a single wrench, rips it off my wrist amid a spatter of spirit-stuff droplets that resemble blood. Then she holds up the snake and rips off its head in one deft motion. Its body briefly writhes in her grasp before it dissipates, the magic of its existence flowing back to the *quinsatra* where it belongs.

"Well, Dasyra," the Warrior says, looking me in the eye. *"How do you feel?"*

The heart pain in my chest remains, stabbing and undeniable—but the fog in my brain is clearing. I can think again. "Better," I answer, the word a trembling whisper. I lick my dry lips and answer more firmly, "Much better. Thank you."

Then, as though belying my words, the cord wrapped

around my heart suddenly tugs. With a cry, I press my hand to my breast, close my eyes, and clench my teeth.

Even with my eyes closed, I can see the Warrior shake her head—she's part of me, after all. But her faintly amused expression strikes me as unfair given the circumstances.

"*Tell me,*" she says, *"do you honestly believe he means to kill you?"*

I grimace. "He certainly meant to. Otherwise, we wouldn't have begun this journey in the first place."

Ilestriesa shrugs. *"Meant to, perhaps. But now?"*

I don't know. I simply don't know. Now that the spell no longer poisons me, my terrified certainty has faded as well. But do I need a spell to tell me that Lodírhal is dangerous?

The Warrior sits back on her heels and huffs softly, a distinctly annoyed sound. *"You know, I waited many years between vessels before selecting you. The Miphates tried to foist me on any number of worthy candidates. But I refused them all until finally, in desperation, they presented me with you. I took one look at you and thought, 'Ah! Here is something different. She's smart, yes. They're all smart, these Miphates mages. This one, however, is also sensitive. Intuitive. And not at all vicious.' These are strengths I never possessed in life. Strengths I knew I would need if I was ever to be free."*

"Free?" I look up, momentarily surprised enough to forget my pain. "You . . . you're a prisoner?"

The Warrior rolls her eyes and indicates the amulet in my hand with a jut of her chin. *"What do you think?"*

The truth is, I've never considered it. I assumed that Ilestriesa, a warrior through and through, had willingly bound her soul to the amulet for the sake of her people, for the ongoing glory of war. I wonder now what else Ilestriesa might have revealed to me if Mage Jhaan and Mage Glarald had not so strictly controlled my training. After all, I had no idea up until this moment that I could have actual conversations with the spirit for whom I provided material substance.

"Let's not worry about that just now," Ilestriesa says with a quick toss of her head. I wonder that she should bring up the subject of her enslavement only to dismiss it this easily, but her next words immediately distract my attention. *"We must focus on keeping you alive. The longer you are apart from Lodírhal while your Fatebond remains unsealed, the weaker you will become. However, your weakening isn't as extreme as his because you're not fae. Make no mistake, this parting is pure torture to your mate. He cannot survive it long. And if he dies, you won't live much longer."*

My heart sinks to my stomach. I hadn't realized the danger I'd put him in with my wild flight. But then, while the spell had its hold on me, I hadn't realized much of anything. "What can I do?"

"You must go to him. Tell him how you feel. Secure the Fatebond and both your lives."

I shudder. "But what if it's a trick after all? What if he still intends to take me to the Sundering Place and kill me?"

"If it were a trick, he wouldn't have given you his name."

"His name?" A frown knots my brow. "I don't have his name. That is, I almost reached it that first night when he stole me away. But beyond that, he's kept it a careful secret."

There is something singularly disconcerting about being eye-rolled by a spirit warrior. Again. And then she adds, *"For such a smart little thing, you are remarkably dense, my Vessel. Search inside yourself. He* has *given you his name. You possess it even now. And with it, you can find him and fix this bond before it snaps. You can save him. You can save us all."*

I don't believe her. How can I? Surely I would remember if my fae-king bond mate mentioned something so significant in my presence.

But that shining face wears an expression too certain to ignore.

I close my eyes again, bow my head, and reach inside, down to where that cord of connection wraps so tightly around my heart. Reach along the cord, following it deeper, deeper, deeper . . .

My eyes flare open. I stare up at Ilestriesa. Her mouth quirks in a wry smile.

"I have it!" I gasp. "I have his name!"

Then I toss back my head and laugh.

LODÍRHAL

I slip in and out of consciousness. To be awake and aware is excruciating . . . but when I sink back into darkness, the pain there is unimaginably worse. But pain means I'm alive. Which means *she* is alive as well. Somewhere.

I can still save her.

Now and then, I become aware of the rhythm of oars and the gentle undulations of water below me. Kyriakos ordered his people to put me on a litter and carry me through a few layers of reality to where his ships waited. Now we sail that last stretch of the journey to the Sundering Place. No more adventures, no more battles. My sixth peril is the very one who delivers me to my destination. As for my final peril . . . I scowl even as another wave of pain drags me back into perdition.

I am my own final peril. And by far the deadliest.

Time passes. I distantly feel the hours creep by. Daylight swells and fades on the edges of my vision, yielding to night. But day and night, light and darkness mean nothing to me. From now until the end, only greater and lesser degrees of pain exist.

I realize we've stopped. I'm not sure when. It may have happened hours ago. Emerging from the depths of suffering, I blink several times. My vision clarifies until I'm able to see the wafting curtains of the litter for one moment before a hand draws them back.

Kyriakos stands silhouetted in starlight, gazing down at me.

"Well now, my friend," he purrs, tilting his head and inspecting me in all my sweat-drenched, broken humiliation. "Not much left of you now, is there? Gods above, I'd almost be tempted to stick a knife into your heart myself. Fortunately, I'm not such a fool as to forget the curse that accompanies the murder of a king. But . . ." He leans over me, and I feel the hilt of a knife press into my palm. Kyriakos hisses, "The curse cannot touch me if you do the deed of your own volition."

Leaving these poisonous words to burn in my ear, he grips my shoulder and drags me upright. "So, do you still wish to save your little Fatebonded's life? Little time remains to you, and it must be your choice."

I feel . . . not *strength,* exactly . . . more like *determination* flood through my soul and out into my body. Drawing on that, I pull free of Kyriakos's grasp and rise from the litter on which I've lain so helplessly. As I push out onto the open deck of the ship, I see where we have come.

The boat lies in a harbor just off the shore of a harsh landscape. Although the darkness of predawn still claims the world, I see fanglike mountains against a star-strewn sky. Set deep into the side of the nearest mountain is a great stairway, each step carved and shaped to perfection as though by divine design, leading straight up.

Up to the heights above.

Beneath the open sky.

Where the altar stands in full sight of Nornala, goddess of unity.

The Sundering Place.

"You must climb alone." Kyriakos stands at my side, watching me closely, hungrily. "If you lack the strength, you will surely die on that stair, and the Miphata will die as well, wherever she is. If you would spare her life, you must reach the altar stone."

I square my shoulders. Now that the moment for action has arrived, I can fight back despite the intensifying pain. Perhaps the air of this place holds something, some blessing from the goddess herself? Whatever it is, I will use it. I will do what I've come here to do.

Kyriakos smiles again. "True Love," he says, taking a step back. "Never thought I'd see the day when Lodírhal of Aurelis was brought low by such a disease of the heart."

In that moment, I realize the truth: This was Kyriakos's plan all along. My death. Not the Miphata's. *Mine.* Somehow he foresaw this moment, guessed at this weakness in me. And now, like a circling vulture, he prepares to enjoy the spoils of my demise. For when a fae king dies—a rare occurrence in Eledria—the power released from his body is tremendous. Usually his heir is on hand to receive that power, as I was when my father's life ended.

But I have no heir. It is Kyriakos who will receive my life force. And I am helpless to prevent it.

I tighten my grip on the knife. At least my one-time friend had the grace to bring me here and give me a chance to save the girl whose love has killed me. He could have simply waited for me to expire and take my life force then. Yes, he conspired to bring about my end . . . but perhaps a spark of genuine friendship exists in his cold black heart after all.

"Go on, Lodírhal," Kyriakos says. "Dawn is almost upon us."

I nod and square my shoulders. "Lower the shore boat."

DASYRA

*H*olding my Fatebonded's name in my heart, I watch how it opens a path before my feet, one of those strange Hinter Paths I've only ever walked with him. But I'm still with him, in a way, for as long as this connection remains, for as long as I carry his name. With this knowledge in mind, I stride forward with confidence.

This path feels different from the others we've walked, both more perilous and more beautiful. Instead of shadowy forest all around, great expanses and drifting clouds surround me. Here and there they break, and I glimpse stars both above and below me. It is beautiful and dizzying and dangerous. If I allow my gaze to wander, I might easily be lost in that vastness.

Instead, I focus on the path before me. This is what loving someone really means, I realize. This peril. This pain. True beauty cannot exist without either of those risks. But glory may follow as well, and my heart swells with joy at the prospect.

If only I can reach him in time.

Ilestriesa rests within the amulet, which glows warm against my breast. As I walk, I spare a thought for the captive Warrior. Might I possibly save her? Does any way exist to liberate her from this prison? The amulet and I are bonded for life, but my death would be insufficient to free the spirit inside. She could only wait for another vessel to be found.

Yet she chose me for a reason. Is it perhaps because she sees in me the means to her salvation?

I shake my head, pushing these thoughts back down for the time being. I will help Ilestriesa if possible. But first I must find Lodírhal and restore our bond—the only hope of survival for any of us now.

Redoubling my pace, I rush along the path through the cloudy Hinter, my footsteps sure and confident despite the stomach-churning vastness all around. Strange, how comfortable I am with this sort of travel after so short a time. In many ways I feel as though I'm better suited to life in Eledria than I ever was to the narrow confines of existence I experienced back home.

A gate appears before me so suddenly that I only just manage to skid to a stop before colliding with it. Not exactly *visible*, it is nonetheless unmistakable: a churning energy prickles through my awareness. I stretch out one hand, tentatively exploring.

Something resists. Something, or someone, on the other side of that gate does not want me to pass through. My searching fingertips sense expectation and opposition and *power*. Vicious, potent power fights to keep the gate shut and barred. When I press a little harder, that power grows. I set my teeth and throw myself straight at the gate. But the opposing force resists my soul, causing me to stagger back and sit down hard on the Hinter path, gasping for breath.

"All right then," I mutter, setting my teeth. "If that's how you want to play."

My hand closes around the amulet. Ilestriesa burns inside, ready to answer my call. I run my fingers along the stone-carved spell, speaking the words in my mind, calling the Warrior up inside me. She rises, looms, her essence blazing bright in this strange atmosphere.

I rise, my limbs surrounded by the Warrior. I could easily let my whole awareness be subsumed into hers, but when I resist that pull, she doesn't fight me. We share this space of existence: her power, my mind.

"All right then," I say once more, facing that gate. "Let's see what you can do against *this.*"

I hurtle forward. The entire force of Ilestriesa's summoned strength strikes that gate, that resistance. A cold shudder ripples into my soul, piercing even the protective layer of the Warrior's spirit. I gasp but keep on pushing until at last I pierce the resistance and fall through realities.

My feet stagger in shallow water. My skirts tangle about my legs, and I stumble, dropping to my hands and knees with water up to my elbows. I taste salt in the air, and when I look up, I see mountains under starlight, edged with the faintest tint of dawn's glow.

I'm through. I don't know where I've arrived, but I'm off the Hinter Path.

And Lodírhal? Is he here? Is he—

Instinct that does not belong to me forces my body into motion before I recognize my own danger. Something sharp whistles past my ear. Surrounded by Ilestriesa's essence, I roll, and the water closes over my head. I surface, gasp for breath, and surge to my feet. My arms rise above my head, and when I bring them back down, Ilestriesa's two bright axes flash into being.

Only then, peering out through the spirit-stuff around me, do I see Kyriakos standing on the beach, sword in hand.

"Welcome, little Miphata," he says, though his gaze is fixed on Ilestriesa's face a good two feet above mine. "I didn't expect to see you here. But then, come to think of it, it's only fitting."

Ilestriesa twirls her axes and takes a menacing step through the shallows. *"Where is Lodírhal?"* I demand, shouting through the Warrior's mouth.

Kyriakos smiles. "You're too late, I'm afraid. He's well on his way to the Sundering Place. You'll never reach him in time. Not if I have anything to say about it."

Though I know I shouldn't look away from him for even a moment, I look up to the stairway carved into the mountain behind him, rising so sharp and steep into the pinking darkness. And there, partway up . . . is that Lodírhal climbing those stairs with swift, sure strides as though pursued by the very hounds of death?

I open my mouth. His True Name is on my tongue, ready to be cried out.

Then Kyriakos is upon me, his great sword swinging. Ilestriesa blocks his blow with a swoop of her left-hand ax. Her right ax lashes out, but he dances just out of reach, his long dark hair fanning the air behind him.

"Come now, Ilestriesa!" he cries, his dark voice brimming with manic laughter. "Is that all you've got?"

LODÍRHAL

I feel the hugeness of the drop behind me as I scale the mountain stair. I don't dare look back. If I did, I'd lose what little courage remains to me. Even so, I feel it, and the sensation of that great emptiness threatens to turn my knees to water.

Strangely, the pain in my heart lessens as I approach my goal. Perhaps Nornala sees my plight and has taken pity.

I climb onward, often leaning forward to use my hands to pull myself up one step after another. This climb feels endless, a stairway to the very heavens. The sky arcing overhead turns pink with coming dawn. I must reach my destination before the sun rises. I must perform the sacred sacrifice and liberate my Fatebonded once and for all.

I clutch Kyriakos's knife in my right hand. The blade rings loud against stone as I climb.

By the time I reach the uppermost height of that stair,

sweat pours down my face and body, drenching my shirt. But the altar stands before me, a great white stone carved with intricate patterns of knots. Unity knots, never meant to be undone.

My limbs tremble with dread and vertigo as I pull myself toward that altar. Raising my free hand, I grasp the top of the slab and pull myself up until I can rest my head against the cool stone and close my eyes, as though pillowed on softest silk. My breath sighs from my lips in something like a prayer. I've made it! The journey is behind me and that last terrible climb. Only the final peril remains to be faced.

After everything else I've done, this, at least, should be simple.

"Nornala," I breathe, lifting my head to gaze up to the mountain rising above the altar. A halo glow of swelling sunrise silhouettes its peak. "Nornala, in humble gratitude, I offer my thanks for the Fatebinding which has brought me to this place. Although I must now break that binding by the offering of my blood, I am glad to have known it, the most precious gift of my existence. For this, be you honored and praised."

With the final words still trembling on my lips, I climb onto the altar and kneel in the center of the stone. In the center of the most intricate knot. Briefly I look down between my knees at the delicate twists and turns of the carving, at all the little grooves into which my blood will pool as it spills from my dying body.

I close my eyes, raise the dagger. I know exactly how to thrust it up under the ribs so that it finds the heart in a single swift motion. I've done it many times on the battlefield.

"Nornala," I say, "accept the price of my blood in this moment of sundering and set her free."

The bright blade flashes in the first rays of the rising sun as I plunge it true.

DASYRA

*K*yriakos charges straight at us. At the last possible instant, he feints to the right, then shifts his weight nimbly to the left, lashing out with the greater reach of his blade.

Ilestriesa doesn't fall for the feint. Too fast for him, she slams her right-hand ax down on his sword, momentarily plunging it under the salty shallows we're standing in. But Kyriakos is already in motion, using the momentum of his swing to lift his body high in the air and kick. His heel connects with her jaw.

And I feel it. I am deep down inside the projected spirit of the Warrior, yet his blow seems to strike me. Knocked off balance, I stagger and fall to my hands and knees in the water. Here lies the danger in denying Ilestriesa full control: She is ready and able to sustain such blows, but I am less resilient. Darkness and agonized sparks explode in my head.

Yet Ilestriesa is not to be vanquished. I feel her all around me, recovering much faster than I ever could, her battle instincts responsive in ways I cannot fathom. Sensing the whistling steel of Kyriakos's sword aimed for her neck, she raises her arm in time to block the blow, then surges from her knees to her feet, dragging me along with her. Her second ax thrusts forward, its pointed head aimed at our enemy's gut.

Kyriakos is only just quick enough to dance back out of range, his feet splashing from the shallows onto the shore. My jaw still throbs, but my vision clears, and when I peer through the spirit-substance around me, I glimpse my enemy's flashing grin.

"Dawn is upon us, Miphata," he cries, speaking directly to me. "Behold!" He sweeps one hand, drawing my gaze up to the sky streaked with golden beams as the sun crests the mountains.

In that same moment, I feel it.

A blow to my heart, like a dagger plunged deep.

Lodírhal.

Lodírhal!

I scream, both hands pressed to my bosom even as the Warrior stands around me with her axes upraised. I close my eyes, grind my teeth, and scream his True Name deep in my soul. I feel him break away from me, falling, falling, falling . . .

"Now," Kyriakos says, his voice a cold laugh, "I will take the power of Aurelis's king. And I will become—"

He never finishes.

My eyes blaze open, and I see the world through Ilestriesa's gaze. I see Kyriakos—his smiles, his laughter, his cruelty, his malice. This man, this creature, who has sought with all his might to end the life of my love.

In a storm of blistering magic, I lunge at him. The Warrior's left ax knocks his blade spinning from his hand even as her right hand catches him by the throat and lifts him off his feet to dangle like a pathetic kitten before her. She chokes the sound of his scream before it can escape his lips. He tries to struggle, but I now pour everything into that grasp. Ilestriesa stands unhindered by her Vessel, a figure of utmost power and dread.

She wants to kill him.

She is going to kill him.

And I . . . I want her to do it.

I want her to shake him so hard that his neck snaps between her fingers, then drop him to the ground and grind his limp and broken body beneath her heels.

I stare through her gaze into Kyriakos's dark eyes. They spark with defiance, but he cannot disguise the fear radiating from his soul. In that moment, I know he is mine. Not Ilestriesa's—*mine*. And I am strong and terrible.

But am I strong enough?

Grief vibrates in every corner of my spirit. I reach for the broken strands of the Fatebond cord but cannot find them. This pain is beyond anything I'd thought possible. But is it enough to make me forget who I am?

My love for Lodírhal is not who I am.

Though I love him—love him with all the longing of the lonely worlds—I cannot lose myself in the sorrow of his loss.

"Dasyra." Ilestriesa's voice whispers in my head. *"Dasyra, what would you have me do?"*

I close my eyes, trying to black out the sight of my

enemy's face, willing myself to offer pain and suffering in return for the pain and suffering given. But I cannot do it.

"Let him go, Ilestriesa," I say.

The Warrior draws back her arm.

Then she hurls the Lord of Ninthalor through the air in a great arc. With a thin cry, he speeds like an arrow out over the water to land with a distant splash not far from where a black-sailed ship lies moored. I watch until his head breaks the water's surface and little figures scramble along the ship's deck, their shouts faint from that distance. Only then do I turn back to face the long stair.

I look up. All the way to the top where the golden light of dawn spills across the world. From that distance, I cannot see what waits above me.

"I'm coming, my love," I whisper. Though I know I'm already too late.

With the might of Ilestriesa burning through me, I run for the stair.

LODÍRHAL

I watch my life's blood flow out from my body and into the grooves in the altar stone. The pain is excruciating but no worse than the pain I've endured since my Fatebonded left me. And through this pain, I know she will be spared. So I don't resent it. I don't try to hide from it.

I lie with my face pressed into the altar, watching the blue trickle of blood make its way through the carved knots to the edge of the stone. With every drop that flows, I feel the threads of the binding cord breaking, unraveling. Soon . . . soon now, she will be free . . .

My vision darkens. My eyes grow heavy. But I am Lodírhal, King of Aurelis. I will not die until the last of my blood has left my body. I must remain here and endure these excruciating moments. Even if I lose consciousness, my soul will stay, observing until the end.

"Respen!"

I try to glower, a reflex from back when this husk of a body still belonged to me. I lack the strength to perform even such a simple action now. But my soul tenses, growing more alert.

"Respen!"

Whose is that voice? Who should call that name? The name known to none but my long-departed mother. That secret name which I hold safe and close.

Suddenly, a burst of white light explodes before my dimmed gaze. A great, blazing figure appears at the top of the stair—seven feet tall, crowned in a glory of shining hair, her dark face set with brilliant pale eyes. She looks straight at me, and those eyes widen.

The vision melts away. And standing in her place . . .

She came.

She came.

I try to lift my hand. But I've lost too much blood. I cannot move. I cannot do anything. I cannot even think to question why she is here now. I can only drink in the sight of her as darkness closes in around me.

A cry bursts from her lips. She rushes to the altar and climbs up, the sacrificial blood soaking into her skirts. Her slim arms catch hold of me, and she must draw on the Warrior's strength to turn me over.

"No, no, no," she whimpers when she sees the knife protruding from my chest. Her fingers grasp its hilt, and she hesitates. I want to warn her that pulling it free will only let the blood flow faster. But it's no use; I have no control of my tongue.

"Respen," she says, gazing into my eyes, searching for some sign of life. Does she know that I can still, for another few moments at least, see her? That the mere sight of her lovely face so stricken with grief is both agony and ecstasy to my soul. "Respen, why? Why did you do it? Why did you not wait for me? I was a fool. I fell for Kyriakos's trick and believed the worst of you. But I'm here now. I never . . . I couldn't . . ."

She bows her head, pressing my face against her bosom, and weeps into the top of my head. I feel her tears on my face, and the sensation is more delight than I ever deserved. Then she tilts her head back, still holding me to her heart.

"Nornala!" she cries. "Nornala, hear me: Do not sever this bond. By your grace, restore it and restore him to me. I beg of you, here in this sacred place, to honor the unity you ordained for our fates. Let our lives be bound together."

The darkness is complete now, my vision utterly blinded. I let my eyelids fall. Death will come soon. My blood is mostly spent. The last of it spills into her lap.

But her arms tighten around me.

"If a life must be taken now that the offering is begun . . . Nornala, will you accept this life of mine instead?"

What? No! No, I did not come all this way so that she should be lost. I am beyond all hopes or desires save for the wish that she should live. I shall go willingly to whatever final destination the gods have for me if only I know that she is well and happy.

Suddenly—light.

I don't know whether I open my eyes, or my spirit somehow witnesses the strange scene unfolding. Perhaps both. Perhaps neither. However it transpires, I see the Warrior. Ilestriesa walks toward me out of the darkness.

She does not look at me; her burning gaze is fixed on the girl in whose arms I lie.

"I always knew you would save me," she says in a voice like cracking doom. *"I always knew you would be the one to end the cycle."*

"But are you sure?" The Miphata's voice echoes from far away. "I cannot ask you to make this sacrifice for me."

"It is no sacrifice," the Warrior responds. *"My time in this world should have ended many long ages ago. So let our lives now be sundered, here at the Sundering Place. I will go in your True Love's stead so that you may complete the binding you are meant to have with him."*

With these words, she bends and plants a kiss on the girl's forehead. For a moment, they gaze into each other's eyes—the warrior and the gentle mage. They are alike and yet so different. I can somehow see the connection between them, as strong as any Fatebond.

The Warrior steps back. *"Go with grace, Dasyra Rolim, my best and final Vessel."*

She stretches out her hand to lift the amulet on its chain around the girl's neck. Her strong fist closes; her wrist twists.

With a crack that shocks through even my dulled senses, the binding breaks. The girl gives a little gasp, and her arms tense around me. Then the whole world fills with golden, glorious song. It blazes through my head, my heart, my soul, and I feel as though my blood has turned to liquid fire running swiftly in reverse of time itself. Somewhere, in a distant place of awareness, I feel hands grip the dagger's hilt and draw it from my chest. I am burning and broken and suddenly so very, very alive.

"Respen?"

I groan and try to lift my eyelids. They're too heavy, so I give up and simply turn toward the warmth against the side of my face, nuzzling closer. I feel the texture of stout fabric, the warmth of a living body, the beat of a heart.

A heart.

Wait . . .

My hand moves. And I'm shocked to realize that I'm the one moving it. When did I regain the ability to control my own limbs? I press my palm against that place in my chest where a gaping knife wound should be. But although I feel torn cloth, beneath it my flesh is firm and whole with only the faintest trace of a scar.

"Respen, can you hear me?"

I know that voice.

Again I attempt to open my eyes, and this time I find the strength, parting my lids to gaze up into that lovely face above me. Into those gray-blue eyes like pools of spring sky, shimmering with tears.

"You," I whisper and lift a trembling hand to touch her cheek with one finger. "You . . . you came back. How . . . how did you . . . ?"

"You gave me your name," she says, cupping my face with her hand. "You gave me your True Name when you gave me that blossom. I'm so sorry, Respen. I'm sorry I didn't understand sooner."

I smile. I cannot help it. The beauty of her face, her voice, her love . . . it's overwhelming. I can do nothing but smile like the lovesick fool that I am.

"Please," I say, my voice strangely hoarse in my throat, "will you tell me your name in return?"

She adjusts her hold on me, bending her face closer until her lips hover just above mine.

"I'm Dasyra," she says.

Then she kisses me.

DASYRA

I crouch at the base of the silver-branch tree and gasp with delight. "Oh, look! Look, they've bonded."

With trembling fingers I touch the delicate blue blossoms entwined together. Green tendrils stretch out from them in all directions, and from those tendrils multiple buds sprout, nearly ready to bloom. I can see the shining blue of their magic centers through the delicate green sepals.

I sit back on my heels, shaking my head. My respenia blossom, which had been so near death, is whole and healthy, wrapped in the embrace of its mate. Their offspring will soon blossom and begin their own individual lives, finding mates and spreading out across this fair valley. But the two in the center are mine. They will come with me when the time is right.

"Are you happy, Dasyra?"

A shiver of pleasure races down my spine at the

sound of that golden voice speaking my name. Rising, I turn to face Respen Lodírhal, my Fatebonded. My husband.

When we climbed down from the altar, holding each other's hands, we took the opportunity to kneel and speak our vows of undying love and loyalty under the watching eyes of Nornala. Later we will reaffirm those vows before witnesses, but that will be a mere formality. The truth of our binding, of our marriage, is already fixed in our hearts.

I stretch out my hand, and Respen entwines his fingers with mine. Many dangers lie ahead of us, I'm sure. Kyriakos is not dead; his ship was gone before we made our way back down the mountain stair. He lives on in all his malice, brooding on ways to take revenge. And I no longer have Ilestriesa's power to protect me. I left the amulet of the Warrior on Nornala's altar, its stone broken in two, the spell-writing shattered.

But I gaze up into my husband's face with confidence. I no longer need Ilestriesa. In truth, I never needed her. We helped each other, yes, but I am strong without her. Strong in my own way . . . with a strength that compliments that of my Fatebonded.

"Yes, my love," I answer his question, stepping toward him. His arm slips around me, and I rest my head against his chest, right over that torn place where the wicked dagger pierced his shirt. I close my eyes, listening to the beat of his living heart. "I am happy."

Then I laugh suddenly, a foolish giggle that I'm not quick enough to suppress.

"What?" my husband asks. His cheek presses against the top of my head. "Why do you laugh, little wife?"

"Oh, nothing." I pull back, my eyes dancing, my mouth unable to stop smiling. "It's just . . . *Respen*. It's a funny kind of name when you think of it. Like a fellow from my world being called *Daisy* or *Rosie*."

He blinks, his brow faintly puckered. "And this is . . . amusing to you?"

I shake my head, laughing again. "Never mind. The name suits you perfectly. I love it."

"Say it again then," he says, his eyes meeting mine. They glow with such heat, I feel a fire lighting in my gut. "Say my name, Dasyra. I want to hear it on your lips again. Say it and tell me what you wish of me."

"Respen." I swallow, my throat suddenly dry and tight. "Respen, I wish for you to kiss me."

He cups my face in his hands and draws my mouth to his. His lips are gentle at first, but when I wrap my arms around his neck, he deepens the kiss. A growl rumbles in his throat, and the sound seems to vibrate down to my gut, making me wild with needs I've never known before.

He draws back before I am ready. I gaze up at him, my breath coming in short, sharp gasps. "What's next?" I ask, scarcely able to form the words.

"Next, my love," my husband says, "we live happily ever after."

I catch his face and pull him down to me again, kissing him harder than before. A little scream bubbles in my throat when he scoops me suddenly off my feet. I cling to his neck, laughing again, as he carries me to where the grass is soft beneath the shade of the silver-branch tree. There he lays me down, and we crush the sweet grass beneath us until its perfume fills the air.

THE END

Don't miss the next STOLEN BRIDES OF THE FAE book!

COLLECT THE ENTIRE STOLEN BRIDES
OF THE FAE SERIES!

Read these books in any order for swoon-worthy romance,
heart-stopping adventure, and guaranteed happily-ever-afters!

You can find them all at www.stolenbrides.com

A NOTE FROM THE AUTHOR

Thank you so much for taking the time to read *Stolen Mage Bride.* I enjoyed every minute of writing this romantic adventure, and I hope it was a lovely escape for you as well.

Reviews are so important to an independent author like me, so if you would take a moment to leave an honest review on Amazon, I would be so grateful! Each review is like gold to me, so I hope you'll consider helping me out.

If you enjoyed this story, I hope you'll check out my other fae romance, *The Moonfire Bride,* featuring a stolen bride, a doomed fae lord, and a marriage bargain that may or may not result in true love.

Or if you're curious to find out what happens to Kyriakos from this adventure, he features as a main antagonist in my Beauty and the Beast trilogy, *The Scarred Mage of Roseward.*

Want to find out more about Dasyra and Lodírhal? Don't miss my upcoming new series, Prince of the

Doomed City, starring their son, Castien. Book 1, *Entranced,* is coming this July.

Happy reading,

Sylvia Mercedes

ABOUT THE AUTHOR

Sylvia Mercedes makes her home in the idyllic North Carolina countryside with her handsome husband, numerous small children, and the feline duo affectionately known as the Fluffy Brothers. When she's not writing she's . . . okay, let's be honest. When she's not writing, she's running around after her kids, cleaning up glitter, trying to plan healthy-ish meals, and wondering where she left her phone. In between, she reads a steady diet of fantasy novels.

But mostly she's writing.

After a short career in Traditional Publishing (under a different name), Sylvia decided to take the plunge into the Indie Publishing World and is enjoying every minute of it. She's the author of the acclaimed Venatrix Chronicles, as well as The Scarred Mage of Roseward trilogy, and the romantic fantasy duology, Of Candlelight and Shadows.

ACKNOWLEDGMENTS

The Stolen Brides of the Fae series could not have come together without the combined efforts of each of the wonderful authors. So let me take a moment to thank them for their contributions.

First, thank you to Emma Hamm for being willing to *go first.* Always an intimidating prospect! But with your usual finesse you rose to the challenge, crafting a story that is not only delightful in its own right, but also serves as a perfect lead-in to all the rest of these romantic adventures. You rock, Emma!

Tara Grayce, I'm pretty sure your optimism, kindness, grace, and good sense held us together through all the ups and downs of pulling this project together. I can only hope every collaboration I participate in has someone like you in it (like, you know . . . the one we're in together later this year!).

I am so glad, SM Gaither, that we had you on board to coordinate our awesome Instagram promo with Books of

Matches Media! Being a total Instagram newbie, it was so great to have your expertise to draw from. And how awesome is it to see all these pretty pictures peppering our feeds every day?

Angela J Ford . . . you are incredible. That website you created for our series is so fantastic. I am in awe of your work. Also, thank you, thank you, thank you for coordinating our cover designs with Dominique Wesson! I don't think we could have had prettier covers for this series if we'd bargained with the fae for them.

Clare Sager, you are undoubtedly one of the most generous people I know. You volunteered your time and expertise to format all of these books for us, and the result is so pretty. Thank you so much for stepping in and helping us achieve that next level of polish.

Oh gracious, Kenley Davidson, I don't know what we would have done without you to deal with all the behind-the-scenes Amazon STUFF. Seriously, I had no idea how complicated it would be to get some of those coordination details ironed out . . . but you tackled it all like a champion and saved our series. Thank you from the depths of my heart.

And Sarah K.L. Wilson, this series would not be what it is today without your gorgeous typography skills. Thank you for going above and beyond creating the titles for covers, the stand-in pre-order covers, and all the other beautiful images for Instagram and promotions. Your artistry combined with Dominique's paintings make for one of the most beautiful series I've ever seen!

I can't tell you ladies what an honor it was to participate in a collaboration like this with so many of my most-admired names in the indie publishing world. I am so proud of what we've achieved together and can't wait to see all of your books proudly lining my bookshelf.

Hugs,

Sylvia

Printed in Great Britain
by Amazon